THE POPULARITY PLAN

Charlene reached across the table and grabbed Frannie's wrist.

"You're not quitting, do you understand me? This is only the beginning, Fran," she said in a low, threatening voice. "You've got Gary Houseman's attention now. He's not going to forget you. Neither is Shawn McNeil. You may not notice it, but already *The Plan* is working. Give it a chance—I know you'll be glad you did."

The Popularity Plan

Rosemary Vernon

BANTAM BOOKS
Toronto · New York · London · Sydney

RL 5, IL age 11 and up

THE POPULARITY PLAN
A Bantam Book/September 1981
Sweet Dreams is a Trademark of Bantam Books, Inc.

Cover by Pat Hill

ISBN 0-553-20325-8

Published simultaneously in the United States and Canada

Bantam Books are published by Bantam Books, Inc. Its trade-mark, consisting of the words "Bantam Books" and the por-trayal of a bantam, is Registered in U.S. Patent and Trademark Office and in other countries, Marca Registrada. Bantam Books, Inc., 666 Fifth Avenue, New York, New York 10103.

Printed and bound in Great Britain by
Cox & Wyman Ltd, Reading

Chapter One

"I shouldn't have come," Frannie Bronson muttered miserably, her wide-set blue eyes sweeping the dark high school full of dancing couples.

Charlene McDaniels, Frannie's best friend, elbowed her in the ribs. "Don't be silly, Fran. How do you expect guys to notice you if you never go anywhere?"

Frannie frowned. "I still say it's a dumb idea, Charlene. You know how stupid I am around boys. I'm—"

"Excuse me. Would you like to dance?"

Frannie didn't bother to turn and look at the boy who asked that question. He wasn't talking to her, of course. He was talking to Charlene. Gorgeous, curly-haired, petite Charlene, *not me*, she thought with a trace of envy.

Charlene was making a face at her, no, several faces. Actually, Frannie thought she looked like she was going into convulsions.

"Frannie!" Charlene hissed through her teeth.

The boy was looking intently at Frannie, waiting for an answer. Frannie still had her eyes glued to her girlfriend.

"Yes, I'm sure she would love to dance," Charlene announced quickly, pushing Frannie forward until she stood next to the tall, lanky boy. When she finally turned to face him, she saw that he looked decidedly uncomfortable.

Frannie was a bundle of nerves. *What am I going to do? I can't talk—can't even dance!* To make matters worse, the dance was a slow one, and Frannie was sure she'd trample all over his feet.

When the boy smiled down at her, Frannie noticed how good-looking he was—sandy brown hair, friendly brown eyes, a few freckles. He took her hand and led her out to the dance floor. He was a full head taller than she was, and she had to stand on her tiptoes to dance with him. It only made her feel more awkward.

"What's your name?" he inquired. "Mine's Ben."

Frannie cleared her throat.

"What did you say? I didn't catch that," Ben said.

She tried again, but the word just squeaked out, "Frances."

"Huh?"

"Frances," she said a little louder. The music stopped and they moved apart. Frannie couldn't make herself look at Ben, so she concentrated on the floor.

"Nancy, that's a nice name," Ben said agreeably.

Frannie didn't have the nerve to correct him. It had been difficult enough to open her mouth in the first place.

"I've never seen you around school before," he told her.

Frannie could feel herself blushing. Thankfully,

the music started again, filling in for conversation. She could hear her own breathing as he held her, and she concentrated all her energy into following his steps. As usual, she was at a loss for words, and it didn't surprise her one bit when Ben said stiffly, "Seeya around," at the end of the song. He quickly walked across the dance floor to join a group of people near the band.

Neither did Frannie waste any time getting back to the corner where she and Charlene had been standing. She didn't want to be caught in the middle of the dance floor without a partner.

Charlene was talking to Jason Billings, captain of Lincoln High's football team, a boy she'd had her eye on for a few weeks. How did she do it? Frannie wondered. I can barely tell a boy my name, let alone talk to one so casually like that. Now Charlene was laughing, walking away from Jason, while he watched her go. The boys didn't just say "Seeya around" to her.

"Well, how'd it go with the string bean?" Charlene asked, her eyes glinting mischievously.

Frannie shrugged. "Okay."

"That's all?" Charlene probed. "What'd he say to you?"

"He asked me my name. I managed to answer, but he got it wrong. His name is Ben. So much for conversation."

"Aw, all you need is experience, Fran. You've been in hiding for too long."

"Oh, face it, Charlene. I'm just not a talker. I'm hopeless. I go blank when a guy says hello. I want to go home."

"I'm driving. You have to wait until I'm ready to

take you," Charlene reminded her. Jason Billings sauntered back over, took Charlene's hand and led her onto the floor for another slow dance. Frannie watched as the two of them glided gracefully across the floor.

Her heart ached. They looked so wonderful together on that dance floor, real naturals. So did another good friend of hers, Patti Davis, who was dancing with her boyfriend, Scott. Vivacious, outspoken Valerie Sanders, also a friend of Frannie's, was talking animatedly to a group of boys by the refreshments. More than ever, Frannie regretted coming to this dance. She wished Charlene hadn't talked her into it.

"Come on, Fran. What're you going to do instead—sit home and watch the tube?" She had teased, knowing full well that was what Frannie usually did on a Friday night.

"No, I think I might go to a movie," Frannie countered.

"All by yourself?"

"I've been to movies by myself before," Frannie was forced to admit. She often went to the movies alone, or with her parents. But lately, she hadn't been going. It was depressing listening to couples talking and exchanging confidences all around her. The sweet closeness they shared, sitting in the dark theater together, was something she longed for as well. But it seemed to be an impossible dream.

"It's crazy, Fran. Every weekend you sit home, while all your friends have dates, or someplace to go. You never go *anywhere*. Don't you feel a little weird?" Charlene pointed a coral-painted finger-nail at her, and Frannie squirmed uncomfortably.

"A little weird, yes, I guess so," she admitted. Then, thinking of the long nights, alone with her parents, listening to the monotonous click of her mom's knitting needles and watching her dad puffing on his pipe, she knew she was in need of some change. "Oh, all right," she consented final-ly. "I'll go with you."

But this was far worse than sitting at home watching TV, Frannie now thought. She patted her sunshine-blond hair, cut fashionably to high-light her face, and wondered if she looked okay. Of average height, she was lucky enough never to have to worry about her weight. Her pale blue eyes were large and round and her nose, which Frannie insisted was far too narrow, turned gently upward. Charlene described her as having a Nordic look, especially with the new haircut, but then Charlene was *always* trying to make her feel good about herself. The truth was, Frannie was pretty, although she did nothing to play up her looks. Her problem was that she was so shy that every time any boy approached her, she went completely speechless.

Tim Weston, a serious-looking boy who was in Frannie's math class, walked over to her. "Would you like to dance?" he asked, tossing his head to flip his long brown hair out of his eyes.

"No!" The word came out abruptly, rudely, and Frannie instantly wished she could stuff it back into her mouth. "I—I mean, sorry, thank you for asking me."

Tim's lower lip quivered slightly. Frannie knew she had upset him, but he simply said: "Yeah, okay, some other time," and hurried off.

Frannie felt sick. Why did she say that? She wished she could have been tactful, at least. It wasn't Tim's fault she was too shy to speak.

At that moment Charlene wove her way across the dance floor. Oh, no, now Charlene's going to chew me out, Frannie thought.

"You're still standing here?" she asked in amazement. Charlene's dark hair coiled in tight little ringlets across her forehead where she'd been perspiring. "I thought you'd be dancing with Timmy." The twinkle in her dark brown eyes betrayed Charlene's little scheme.

Frannie took a deep breath. "I didn't feel like it, Char. Now will you please stop trying to fix me up?"

The room exploded with the rapid-fire beat of a disco tune which drove nearly everyone onto the dance floor. "No, I won't," Charlene shouted above the noise. She whirled off toward the crowd.

Frannie watched her friend enjoying herself. What is it like to be popular, always having something to say, she wondered wistfully. Ever since she could remember, she had been the shyest kid in her class. As a toddler she had hidden her face in her mother's skirts every time anyone said hello. Teachers always commented on it, and on every report card there was a remark such as, "Frances is an excellent student, but she is such a shy girl. I do wish I could get to know her!"

Being shy as a child was one thing, but when

she became a teenager, shyness turned out to be a really big problem. Here she was in high school, expected to learn a whole set of new rules for relating to boys, gaining friends and being social, and she was a big bust at it. She was already past her sixteenth birthday and still had never been on a date. All because she was still shy—too shy for her own good.

Frannie's parents, especially her mother, were largely to blame. They did everything for her—arranged dentist and doctor's appointments, accompanied her nearly everywhere, solved all her problems (of which she didn't have too many), served as her mouthpieces when she was too afraid to ask for help in stores and made important decisions for her. Until Charlene came along, Frannie accepted their sheltering as totally normal parent behavior.

"Why can't you do things for yourself?" Charlene demanded of Frannie. "You can't let your parents wipe your nose forever, Fran."

"My parents love me," she protested weakly. But Charlene pooh-poohed that and told her it was time to grow up. Deep down Frannie knew Charlene was right and that she was overly protected.

Home life for Charlene was a lot different than for Frannie. In fact, their friendship had begun one day after school in the eighth grade, when the achingly sorrowful sound of someone crying echoed through the long, empty hallways. Frannie discovered Charlene with her head in her locker, crying her heart out. Immediately she set down her books and somewhat timidly lay one hand on Charlene's quaking shoulder. "What happened to you?" she had asked.

Charlene swiped at her eyes with the back of her arm. A dark tendril of her curly hair, loosed from its pony tail, coiled beneath her chin, "I don't know if you'd understand this—I can't really talk to anyone about it," she sniffled. "My parents are splitting up. Big deal, huh? Everyone's parents do it—why am I upset?"

Frannie didn't know how to comfort her. Her heart went out to this girl, whom she'd seen around junior high quite often. She was a fairly popular girl who always had a cute boyfriend—she certainly was not someone you'd expect to find in tears, alone, after school. "I'd be pretty upset if my parents split up," Frannie offered sympathetically, rubbing Charlene's shoulder.

Charlene's doe-brown eyes were bright with tears, but she managed a small smile. "Thanks, I bet you would, too." She turned back to her locker then and rummaged through the books. "You know, you never think it's going to happen to you. Always to someone else, but never you."

"I know," Frannie agreed. She *didn't* know, but just the thought of her parents divorcing gave her butterflies in her stomach. Her parents were like cheeseburgers and french fries as far as she was concerned—an inseparable combination.

Charlene lived only three blocks away from Frannie, so they walked home together. When it was time to say goodbye, Frannie asked, "Are you okay now?"

"Sure, I'm fine," Charlene answered, her voice

still a little shaky. "Please don't tell anyone about this, will you?"

Frannie gasped in surprise. "Of course I won't. You can count on me."

Frannie had kept her word, and a special friendship sprouted from that one confidence. She remained sympathetic during the following hectic months as Charlene weathered her family's breakup. Charlene introduced Frannie to her friends Patti Davis and Valerie Sanders, both popular, talkative girls. Their friendship grew and continued after they entered high school.

Frannie enjoyed their company and liked being included in their conversations about romance and social events. It was almost as if it was happening to her too. She could close her eyes and imagine herself dating football players, participating in after-school clubs, and having people running up to her in the halls. She was seeing what it was like to be popular; unfortunately, none of it rubbed off on her. To the boys she remained invisible.

Tired of warming her little corner of the auditorium, Frannie went over to the restroom. A tall, slender girl bent over the sink, carefully applying eyeliner. Her friend, a cute-looking girl named Lucy, was doing all the talking.

"Did you see Adam look at me? *Did you see?*"

"Yes, I saw," came the tall girl's distracted reply.

"I hope he asks me out," Lucy twittered gaily, pulling a comb through her long, shiny black hair.

"He will, Lucy," said the friend as she turned from her reflection to roll her eyes expressively at Lucy. Both of them burst into a fit of giggles.

Frannie found an unoccupied corner of the mirror and quickly dabbed on some lipstick and checked her hair. She left before either of the girls noticed her.

Outside, a couple strolled hand in hand, silhouetted against the yellow glow coming from the auditorium. There was sudden movement in one dark corner, and Frannie turned and saw a pair with arms entwined, the boy whispering into the girl's ear.

Frannie sighed and moved on. Romance was everywhere. It swirled around her, wafted out from the auditorium in the form of music and happy chatter. She felt so alone. Everyone had someone—everyone, that is, except her.

She rounded the corner, the sounds of the dance fading behind her. A lone figure emerged from the darkness.

"Hi," a male voice said as they neared one another.

Frannie recognized him as Ronnie Schell, a quiet, dark-haired boy who sat in the back of her Art class. The darkness eclipsed a good part of him, making him appear somewhat mysterious, but outlining the narrowness of his face.

"Oh, hi," she responded without hesitation, her eyes meeting his gray ones. Their shoulders brushed ever so slightly in passing one another. Frannie wondered what he was doing around school at night. He never said a word in class. In that way he was sort of like herself. She had, in fact, noticed his artwork in more detail than she had ever noticed him—until this moment.

Frannie wanted to turn around and see if Ronnie went inside the auditorium, but she didn't want him to catch her looking, so she kept her eyes focused straight ahead.

She climbed up on the bleachers overlooking the football field, and sat there for a long time. It was pleasantly deserted, with only the faint thump of dance music in the background. Spotlights sent ghostly beams across the field, but where Frannie sat it was completely dark. She would enjoy hearing about Charlene's good time at the dance, but Frannie couldn't bear to stand and watch everyone dancing, feeling awkward as she always did in similar situations.

As often as Charlene had confided in Frannie, Frannie had never confided much in Charlene. She had never, for instance, told Charlene how much her shyness bothered her. She had some-how convinced her friend that she wasn't inter-ested in boys or dancing, which was why she had never forced her to come to dances until now. But now that she had turned sixteen that excuse didn't work anymore, and Charlene began to put pressure on her to, in her words, "circulate and get out in the world."

Right then and there on the bleachers, Frannie decided this would be the last time Charlene would drag her to a dance, or anything else. Friday nights at home were better than risking ridicule, anyday. Frances Bronson was just not cut out for a busy social life.

"Frannie, I've been looking all over for you!"

Charlene cried, materializing out of the darkness. "Where've you been?" She clomped up the bleachers to where Frannie sat.

"Right here the whole time," Frannie replied, laughing. She pulled her soft, brown sweater over the creme blouse she wore. "Is it time to go?"

Charlene sounded exasperated. "It was time to go fifteen minutes ago."

"Where's Jason?" Frannie asked, recalling the admiring glances he had given Charlene earlier. It wasn't likely that she'd lost him that easily.

"Oh, he wanted to give me a ride home, but I told him I came with you, so I'd take a rain check."

"Sorry I got in your way," apologized Frannie, thinking how aggravating it must be for Charlene to have to give her a ride home when she'd had the opportunity to ride home with a great guy.

"It's okay, Fran. You weren't in my way." Frannie clambered down the bleachers behind Charlene. "I think you're in your own way."

"What do you mean?" Frannie narrowed her eyes at her friend. "Face it, you blew it tonight. You've got what it takes to get a guy. You're really cute and a great listener. Boys love that." Charlene threw up her hands. "But what do you do? You stand there and spend all your time driving boys away."

"Well, so?" Frannie demanded. How outrageous of Charlene to compliment her and in the same breath remind her what a dud she was in the boy department.

"Well, so..." Charlene bit her lower lip in a gesture of deep concentration. "I think we have to get together and work on your technique."

Chapter Two

"How was the dance?" Frannie's parents chorused when Frannie and Charlene entered the house.

Expectancy was written all over their faces. Frannie sighed. Her parents always made a big deal over everything she did. In a way, it was nice, but sometimes, like now, it bothered her.

Charlene laughed. "Fran, go on, tell them about the dance." She nudged Frannie in the ribs once more. Frannie didn't say a word. "Okay, I'll tell them. Fran was asked to dance two times before she went off to hide."

Frannie groaned. "Charlene!"

"I guess no one there turned you on, huh, Frannie," Mr. Bronson said, beaming in what he thought was his daughter's behalf.

A blonde version of Burt Reynolds was how Charlene pictured Frannie's father. A little heavier, a little older, but still handsome, with slate-blue eyes and a little cleft in his chin.

Frannie certainly didn't inherit her shyness from her father. An outgoing, friendly man, Sam Bronson ran a local advertising agency.

"How about some cocoa, girls?" Mrs. Bronson offered. At forty-one, Joan Bronson was an attractive, ginger-haired woman with a pert, slightly turned-up nose and what appeared to be limit-less energy.

The two girls followed her into the kitchen. Charlene chattered on about Frannie's attitude at the dance while they waited for the milk to warm up.

"I was shy too, when I was young, Charlene," Joan said, placing the cookie jar on the table. "I remember this one boy I thought I was madly in love with. I used to stare at him and daydream. But I never once talked to him, even though I had a crush on him for two years. Can you imagine?"

Frannie interrupted. "Yes, Mom. You've told me that a hundred times."

"*I* haven't heard the story," Charlene piped up. "I can't believe that of *you*, Mrs. Bronson. You're so together."

"It's true," Joan admitted with a chuckle.

Charlene leaned forward across the kitchen table. "So how'd you beat it? I've about given up on Fran."

"I love the way you two discuss me like I was some kind of weirdo," Frannie complained. "Can't we talk about something else?"

"I outgrew my shyness, eventually. When I went away to college, I had to learn to have a certain amount of independence. My mother wasn't around to do everything for me, to be my mouth-piece, make phone calls for me—the things I'd always depended on her to do. The girls in my dorm helped me out, too. They gave me self-confidence lessons."

Frannie's father strolled in and poured himself a cup of coffee. "Your mother wasn't so shy when

I met her," he interjected, and winked at his wife.

A faint blush crept over Joan's cheeks as she continued. "When the girls first started the lessons, they had me carrying on imaginary conversations, pretending I was talking to a young man I liked. It was silly, but it worked. By the time I finished the lessons, I was on my way."

"By the time we met," Mr. Bronson testified, "she was asking the boys out, which was really a switch in those days!"

Mrs. Bronson threw a dish towel at her husband, which missed him by a foot. "I was *not*, Sam. Now cut it out."

The girls burst into giggles as the two playfully flung the dish towel back and forth across the kitchen.

"No one would believe this lovely, self-assured department store buyer was once a shrinking violet, now would they?" Sam teased, spinning the dish towel above his head lasso-fashion.

"You two are crazy!" Frannie exclaimed, shaking her head in amazement. Honestly, sometimes her parents embarrassed her, acting like little kids. She caught Charlene watching her parents longingly, probably wishing the same good feeling prevailed in her own house, Frannie thought.

"Let's go in your room," Charlene suggested abruptly. "I want to see those pillows you made."

"Sure." Frannie led the way into her bedroom.

Frannie had hand-picked the furnishings for her room very carefully. She enjoyed decorating a lot and was even considering becoming a decorator when she got older. She and her mother had found bargain furniture at garage sales and flea markets. There was a table which Frannie had antiqued in blue, and a little desk with a matching chair she had stained in oak after stripping off layer upon layer of paint.

Frannie had made her own quilt, too, a vertically striped masterpiece in green, blue and creme— the same colors as the new throw pillows she had recently completed. She'd borrowed the color scheme from a window display at Sempel's, the store where her mother worked.

"I love these pillows, Fran," Charlene picked up one with a triangle arrangement of patchwork. "How do you do it?"

Frannie shrugged, switched on the TV, moved a pile of clothes from bed to chair and flopped down on the mattress. "Aw, it's no big deal. I like making things."

Charlene rearranged the pillows. "I sure wish I could make something like this. Every time I go near the sewing machine the threads jam up on me."

Frannie laughed. "I guess you're just not the homebody type." She kicked off her shoes.

"You, on the other hand, are too much of a homebody. You're like one of those people who is afraid to leave the house to go to the supermarket. Except you're afraid to deal with boys." Charlene diagnosed her knowingly. "Not to be mean, Fran, but we've got to do something about you—before it's too late."

"Charlene, I wonder why I put up with you," Frannie replied jokingly, stirring her cocoa.

"Remember the time Bryan Schofield came up to you at school and asked you out, and you got all scared, and just turned and ran from him?"

Frannie's stomach churned. She wished Charlene hadn't brought that up. What a dumb thing to do—actually run from a boy! "It was stupid, I know," she agreed in a low voice.

"Your mother gave me an idea." Charlene stared at the TV screen, which was signing off for the night with the *Star Spangled Banner* and a restful ocean scene, before she went on. "You know, what her friends did for her in college doesn't seem like such a bad idea. I wonder why she never tried it with you. I mean, it worked for her, cured her shyness, didn't it?"

Frannie wagged her head. "She did try. Once, when I was fourteen she made me call up this guy, one of her friends' sons. It was awful. When he got on the line, I froze. I was so embarrassed I hung up. I guess Mom was embarrassed too, 'cause she never brought up the subject again. Maybe I'll just have to wait until I get to college."

"That's ridiculous," Charlene said. "Let me think. . . . You know, maybe mothers can't help in situations like this." Charlene moved some cushions and sat next to Frannie on the bed. "Maybe you need a little help from your friends."

"No, I don't," Frannie pouted. "I don't need your help."

"Just look at your mother!" Charlene countered. "Didn't she have her friends help her get over her shyness?" Charlene waited expectantly for her answer.

"Yes, but—"

"If she could do it, why can't you?" Charlene interjected. "She's gone through about the same things as you. You're such a cute, smart girl, it's a shame to have you go to waste."

"Charlene, now you sound like one of my dad's ads. I don't feel like I'm wasting myself," she retorted. "I just don't know how to talk to boys, that's all. I clam up and can't think of anything to say. Or when I do talk, I say something that doesn't make any sense. Let's face it, I'm not the most interesting person in the world, you know." She plumped pillows behind her and lay back. "You can't compare me with Mom, anyhow. She's never been boring."

"Now you're putting yourself down. I think you're wrong. I think 'talking to boys' lessons, or self-confidence lessons, are exactly what you need. It sure couldn't hurt," Charlene argued. "Look at all those books on assertiveness training. 'How To Win' by being this way and that. They've got something to say, or else they wouldn't be published. It must've worked for somebody out there."

Frannie was growing tired of the conversation. "Charlene, I really wish I was more like you, honest. I'd have boyfriends, invitations to parties and dances and picnics—all that stuff. But some people are just born shy. I just have to accept it, that's all."

"You don't have to, don't you see?"

"I don't want my friends to think of me as a problem, either. Stop trying to change me, okay?"

But Charlene only half-heard what Frannie was saying—she already had her own ideas. "We could get boys to talk to you, ease you into conversations gradually so you wouldn't get embarrassed. I just know it could work."

"Charlene, it's a dumb idea. Forget it. I'm always embarrassed, I was *born* embarrassed."

"We could initiate a real plan—something solid—a day-by-day program with a different guy every day, so none of them would get wise to what was happening," Charlene thought aloud, getting more excited by the idea as she went on.

"That's really awful!" Frannie protested adamantly. "There is no way I'm going to do it—no way. Do you think I'd voluntarily want to act like an idiot?"

"C'mon, Fran," Charlene urged. "It won't be bad at all. You've got to learn sometime, and you can't go on like this."

"Why not?" Frannie wanted to know. "I've gotten along just fine so far."

"You call this 'just fine'?" Charlene's hand swept grandly about the room. "Sure you've got your art, your projects, but is that all there is to life?"

"It's enough for right now. I'm just fine, thanks," Frannie drew her knees up to her chest and rested her chin on them, like she used to as a little girl.

Charlene's expression turned stony and her eyes blazed. "Okay, Frannie, if that's how you want it. I think you could be a big success, and I really want to help you. But if you're not ready to help yourself..." She drew a deep, quavering breath. "If you *enjoy* missing out, cutting yourself off from everything I know you really want, then go ahead...stupid." Charlene grabbed her cocoa mug, whirled around and stormed out of the bedroom without a backward glance.

Frannie listened as she heard Charlene say goodnight to her parents and leave.

Never had she seen Charlene so mad before. They had been so close since becoming friends, never having an argument or disagreement of any kind. Frannie felt positively sick. What's wrong with me? she asked herself. Am I as dumb as Charlene says I am? Or doesn't she realize how impossible her suggestions are for someone like me?

The entire weekend stretched ahead of Frannie, long and unexciting. Homework, sewing, reading, listening to records, watching television, how many weekends had she spent that way, knowing that all her friends were out with boyfriends, having a good time?

Chapter Three

All day Saturday and Sunday, Frannie agonized over her argument with Charlene. Charlene's friendship meant so much to her that she couldn't bear to have this anger between them. It was miserable this way—worse, she supposed, than not having a friend at all.

Countless times Frannie reached for the telephone to call her, then changed her mind. If she called, she'd have to go along with that ridiculous plan, for that was all Charlene wanted. And why she was being so pushy about it, Frannie couldn't figure.

Yet it wasn't just the disagreement that bothered Frannie—it was that a lot of what Charlene had said Friday night was true.

Did she really want to spend the rest of her life running from boys who asked her for dates? Did she really want to let her parents speak for her forever? Deep down she knew her folks wouldn't always be around to say, "Our daughter would like an orange soda, please." It was really up to her to learn about dating. Sure, she hated the stupid plan idea, but she also knew Charlene well enough to know she was awfully stubborn, and would stick to her guns on this subject.

And maybe it wasn't that awful, she decided, the more she thought about it.

Finally, at five to four on Sunday afternoon, Frannie called Charlene. She knew she'd be home then because the McDaniels had been eating early on Sundays since Charlene's dad moved out.

"Charlene?" An uncomfortable silence followed. "I—I'm sorry." Somehow those words didn't seem adequate for what Frannie was feeling inside.

"I should think you would be," Charlene returned, the residue of Friday's anger sizzling across the wires.

"I really am. I was wondering..." This was the really hard part, giving in to the very thing she was so against. "About your idea..."

There was a longer silence. Frannie waited. "Charlene? Are you there?"

"Excuse me. I was just picking myself up off the floor." She cleared her throat noisily. "You wouldn't be thinking about the self-confidence idea, would you?"

Frannie grinned. Underneath that haughty, fake tone, she could sense her friend's pleasure. "Yes I am talking about just that."

"I'll call Patti and Valerie and be right over!" Charlene announced, then abruptly hung up.

All three were on the doorstep ten minutes later. Patti Davis, a tall, vivacious brunette, was president of the Speech Club and had absolutely no trouble whatsoever talking to boys (or anyone else for that matter) about anything. She often joked that her destiny was to become a TV talk show host. "Maybe fill in for Johnny Carson sometimes," she said.

Red-haired, bubbly Valerie Sanders was the kind of girl who could always make you laugh, no matter how down you were. "I guess you guys don't know what you call two spiders who just got married?" she asked as they trooped into Frannie's room.

Patti rolled her eyes. "No, I guess we don't," she answered, bracing herself for the punch line.

"Newlywebs."

Everyone groaned. "That's pretty bad, Val," Charlene commented.

"Well, what're we waiting for?" Patti flounced onto the floor, and drew a theme book out from under her arm. "Let's teach this girl how to talk." She made a big production out of opening the book to the first clean, creamy, blue-lined page.

Frannie started to get cold feet. "Hey, Patti, I don't know what you have in mind, with the theme book and—"

"You just leave that up to us," Patti said. "We've got big ideas, and we know what we're doing, don't we girls?" She took a felt-tipped pen out of her pocketbook.

"Of course," Val agreed, sitting lotus style on the swirled carpet. "We're the experts, aren't we?"

"First of all," Patti said as she smoothed the page with her palm, "you need something to say."

"That's the hard part," Charlene put in. "Fran draws a complete blank when anyone asks her her name."

They all groaned.

"My voice just sort of gets stuck in my throat. Sort of like a glob of peanut butter does when you don't have anything to wash it down with. I get too scared, I guess," Frannie explained as she selected a Pink Floyd record and put it on the turntable. "Or else I lose my voice altogether, which makes a guy think I'm stuck up."

"That'll do it," Patti agreed knowingly. "You've got to know how to have a conversation, establish rapport."

"But I'm still on 'hello,' Patti," Frannie reminded her. "I can't get past introductions!"

Val nodded her head. "Ooh, this girl needs help—fast!"

Charlene clapped her hands together sharply. "Okay, girls, now we know where our priorities lie. So what do we do with Fran?"

"First of all," Patti said, "as we all know, she needs self-confidence. She's too shy. She can't say 'hi' to a guy without choking, blushing or croaking the word out. So our priority is to get her to overcome her fear of talking to boys."

"How?" three voices demanded in unison.

"We must have a definite plan," said Patti. "I'm sure you've all got your own ideas?"

"I've been thinking about it all weekend," Charlene admitted, glancing at Frannie, all hostility forgotten. "We have to make her talk to boys, put her in situations where she's forced to open her mouth. I've thought of something like staged 'scenes' she can take part in—subtle situations no boy will ever guess are staged—natural occurrences like..." she hesitated. "It sounds silly, I know, but how about dropping a pencil so that it rolls under a boy's desk?"

Frannie grimaced. Worse than she imagined.

"That's going to do it? How will picking up a pencil make me talk easier?"

"You don't get it, Frannie. You'll whisper 'thank you' and smile mysteriously. In that one quick moment you'll capture interest."

She considered it dubiously. "Seems really weird."

"Of course it does. This is only step one. You must progress from whispering to actual talk. We'll take one day at a time," Charlene beamed.

"Sounds good, Charlene," Patti said. "I'll write that one down for Day One." She printed "Day One" and the strategy next to it in purple ink. "Now we need a boy."

"Is there anyone you like in particular, Frannie?" Val inquired, her eyebrows bobbing up and down comically.

Frannie turned beet red. She had admired many boys from a distance, but never had a crush on any one boy.

"Just pick one," Val urged, and the others giggled.

Frannie thought briefly of Ronnie Schell in her art class, and his bold, exciting drawings that she admired. He was about as shy as herself, and she wouldn't dare embarrass him, so she didn't mention him. "You pick one for me," she told Val, erasing Ronnie's image from her mind. "You have good taste."

Val chuckled. "Okay, we'll choose one for every day of the week, somebody for Monday, another for Tuesday, and so on."

Charlene jumped up. "How about Tim Weston? I'm sure he likes you, Fran."

Tim was the one she had rejected at the dance. "Not him," she said.

"Who sits near you in your classes?" Patti asked.

Frannie had to think for a minute. "Gary Houseman sits in front of me in English."

"Oooh. He's great, and he's not going with anyone, either," said Charlene.

"Gary's perfect," Val agreed with enthusiasm. "How does he sound to you, Frannie?"

Frannie shrugged, overcome by embarrassment. "Okay, I guess." Gary was actually better than "okay." He was cute, and he was not one of those awful teasers who was sure to make her blush. He was a good choice, although she didn't say so to the others.

Patti wrote Gary's name next to "Day One." "Okay, let's go for 'Day Two.' " Patti's idea was to somehow snitch a boy's book, give it to Frannie, and then Frannie would return it to him later (it would be someone Frannie usually saw during the day). "We'll give you lines to memorize, Frannie. Something like, 'I found this book with your name on it.' " She gestured the motion of handing a book to a boy. "He'll say 'thank you,' and you'll smile and say 'you're welcome' and walk away."

"If he asks where you found it, simply say, 'in the main hall.' It's as simple as that," added Val.

"Oh, no, it isn't. I can't stand there in front of a boy reading lines. I'll go blank and forget everything!" Frannie wailed.

Val clapped a hand over her forehead. "You'll memorize, just as you do for English or something. Paste the lines on the closet door, on the inside of your locker, your book, everywhere so

you can't forget. Memorize it like Shakespeare
... 'To be or not to be.' "

"To talk or not to talk," quipped Patti.

Page Garvey was elected for "Day Two" because
Patti had a locker next to his and Frannie had
biology with him. A boy with a locker next to
Frannie was needed for Day Three.

"Fred Brown and Jason Billings are the only
ones I can think of," Frannie told them.

"Jason's mine," Charlene reminded her quickly.
"There're plenty of other boys to practice on."

"Then it's Freddie. He's a nice guy." Patti added
him to the notebook.

Freddie Brown wasn't exactly the greatest-
looking boy in class, but he had a fantastic personality and everyone liked him, including Frannie.

"Drop your books all over the place when Freddie
comes to his locker. He'll have to help you for
sure," Charlene said.

"That's the oldest trick in the book!" exclaimed
Val. "Can't we come up with something more
original than that?"

"Of course it's an old trick," persisted Charlene.
"But it works, doesn't it? What boy won't rush to
the aid of a cute girl?"

"You've got a point there," Patti admitted. "And
it's guaranteed to start a conversation."

" 'Day Four.' Frannie advances to question-
asking stage," Charlene continued, wrapping her
arms around her ankles. "Let me see ... Do you
have weekly tests in something?"

"Art. On Wednesday."

"Okay, on Thursday, just casually ask somebody how he did. No big deal, right?"

"Well, I don't know..." Frannie said.

"Adam Stone is in her art class," Val chimed in, grinning wickedly.

"Adam's a real flirt, Val," Patti put in. "I don't think she's ready for him."

"Yes, but..." Val held up a forefinger and waved it gently in the air. "Adam will notice Frannie. He notices all good-looking girls, and he's charming. Let's face it, any one of us could fall madly in love with Adam at the drop of a hat."

Frannie smiled. Adam Stone was definitely the class Romeo, with black, curly hair, clear skin, compelling tea-brown eyes and the most melting smile she had ever seen on one person. Actually, Frannie thought he was a little *too* good-looking.

"I could drown just in his eyes," admitted Val.

"Okay, now Friday, 'Day Five.' Frannie will lose a homework assignment, and call someone in her class to get it," Patti said.

"I never lose assignments," Frannie told her.

"Pretend, Frannie," Val suggested. "How about biology. If your class is like mine you've got to have weekend homework."

Charlene turned to Frannie. "Who's in that class, besides Page?"

Frannie sent her mind's eye up and down the aisles, choosing boys that were pretty nice and not bad-looking. Jason Steiner, Emmett Caldwell, Bobby Gordon. Bobby was dating someone, Jason was too loud. Emmett sat across from her and would be a good choice. "I guess Emmett Caldwell," she replied. "But I don't like this at all."

"You don't have to like it, Frannie," Charlene

said. "You'll phone him Friday night and just ask him for the weekend assignment."

Frannie's eyes widened in fear. "I have to *call* him on the phone?"

"How else, dummy?" Val giggled. "He doesn't date much, anyway. He's sure to be home."

Frannie tried to hold her terror down so the girls wouldn't see how frightened she was. She wondered if she could possibly be brave enough by Friday to carry it off? Of course not, she couldn't change in a week. "This whole thing is crazy," she blurted out, tears rising in her throat.

"Oh, don't worry about it." Patti patted Frannie's hand. "Now what about 'Week Two'. . . ."

Frannie sat silently as the three girls dreamed up five new schemes for the following week. When they had completed the two-week plan, they handed it to Frannie to paste on her wall.

"These boys are going to think I'm a moron," Frannie commented as she scanned the list. On another sheet Patti was busy composing the lines for Frannie to memorize.

"They won't think anything, believe me," Charlene assured her. "They'll be too busy noticing you."

"Especially if you look super. We'll work on your makeup and hair during the week," Val suggested.

There was a light tap on the door. "Are you girls hungry? You've been in there for over an hour!" Frannie's mother called. "There are brownies in the kitchen when you're ready."

"Mmmm, brownies! There goes my diet," lamented Val, who was slightly overweight. She was always going on different fad diets, then gorging herself as soon as she lost a few pounds. Her weight yo-yoed constantly.

Later that night, after her friends had left, Frannie found an old diary her parents had given her for her fourteenth birthday. It was the five-year kind, but there were few entries in it because she hadn't done much to write about. Until now.

She sat down at her desk and wrote: *"Oct. 12. Today Charlene, Patti and Val came up with a plan to get rid of my shyness and make it easier for me to talk to boys. I am really scared. But if I don't try it, they will hate me, I know it. I couldn't eat my dinner—I felt sick. The plan starts tomorrow. Ugh!"*

Chapter Four

Monday morning, as her friends had suggested, Frannie took special care with her appearance. She set her hair with her mom's electric rollers and put on some eye shadow and mascara she'd borrowed from Charlene. The girls had pointed out that boys should notice her eyes.

Next came the blusher, which Frannie applied a little too liberally and had to wash off. She decided to go without it for now. She did put on some of her mother's cologne, however. Val insisted that boys noticed how you smell.

Usually Frannie stuck to nondescript colors like navy blue and brown, but the girls told her she'd have to start dressing with more pizazz.

So for today she chose a newish pair of dove-gray slacks and a cornflower blue sweater, an outfit she thought looked especially good on her. Granted it was subdued, but as jittery as she felt, she couldn't go to school in something really flashy. That would be awful!

"You look pretty!" exclaimed her father when she walked into the kitchen.

Compliments never failed to embarrass Frannie. She never knew quite what to say, even when they came from her parents. "I do?" she said.

"Sensational," Mr. Bronson reaffirmed.

"What's the occasion, Fran?" her mother inquired, placing a plate of hot buttered muffins on the table.

"Oh, uh . . ." Frannie quickly tried to think of some reason for looking this nice. "Something the girls and I cooked up," she answered, shrugging as if it was no big thing.

Her mother's eyes brightened. "Anybody good-looking?"

Frannie felt ridiculous. She disliked her mother's pointed remarks, but her mother was not easily fooled. She could always see through Frannie as if she were made of tissue paper. "Come on, Mom," she complained.

"Good luck!" Joan spooned scrambled eggs onto each person's plate.

"Mom I'm not very hungry this morning," Frannie held up her hand when the eggs came her way. Her stomach was doing somersaults.

Her mother looked concerned. "Are you feeling okay, Fran?"

Frannie usually had a great appetite in the morning. "Yeah, sure. I'm fine, Mom."

Loud honking outside rescued Frannie from having to pursue the subject. She grabbed her books and purse, threw a kiss to her parents and ran out the front door.

Val was driving her mother's Dodge Dart, picking up Patti, Frannie and Charlene for school. "Hey, look at you!" Val yelled out the half-opened window.

The others whistled as she slid into the back seat. The color rose in Frannie's cheeks. "Hey, what are you, a cheering squad?" she giggled nervously.

"You betcha. We'll be cheering you all the way," Charlene assured her, and Frannie felt Charlene's confidence reach out to her. I wish I felt so sure of myself, Frannie thought, clasping her books tightly against her chest like a shield.

"You'll knock 'em dead today," Patti turned around in the front seat to tell her.

Frannie shook her head. "I hope not. I don't want *that* much attention on me."

"Just in case you forgot." Charlene extracted a shiny red pencil from her canvas purse. "A pencil for Gary."

"Thanks." Frannie took the pencil with a mixture of gratitude and dread. "Thanks a lot."

Arriving at the Lincoln High parking lot, Charlene, Val and Patti scanned the parked cars to see who was already there. Frannie and Charlene had algebra first, so they said goodbye to the others and strolled over to the Math & Science Building, a flat, prefabricated structure that had been added to the overcrowded main building two years ago.

Frannie took her seat and glanced across the room. She'd forgotten Gary Houseman was in this class, too. He sat near the door. A lump formed in her throat just looking at him. He *was* good-looking, with that healthy, sun-kissed look of people who spend a lot of time outdoors, she thought, turning her attention to the uninterrupted expanse of cement out the window.

"Frances, do you think you could unglue yourself from the window and pay attention to the lesson, please?" her teacher, Mr. Randall, asked politely.

Frannie stared at the textbook, blushing, aware that thirty pairs of eyes studied her with interest. This was not the kind of attention she needed. She was a good student and teachers *never* had to ask her to pay attention in class! She wished she were invisible!

After the bell rang Charlene caught up with Frannie, who dashed quickly out of the room. "Whew! I thought you were in trouble for a minute there," Charlene said.

Frannie almost ran alongside Charlene. "I think I'm going to be sick." Her stomach was in full form now, as if it were trying out for the Olympics.

"Just stop worrying, will you? He's only a boy, a real human being, for crying out loud." They stood outside the English class. "Good luck," Charlene said, before running down the hall.

A real human being. That was okay for Charlene to say, but to Frannie, boys were like Martians. What do you say to a Martian?

She took her seat behind Gary Houseman. He wore a checkered shirt and cords. She decided she liked the way his light brown hair curled over the back of his shirt collar.

Mrs. Cummings breezed into the classroom. She was a heavyset woman who favored caftan dresses in exotic colors. Today she was wearing a new Hawaiian print of parrots and jungle scenes.

Frannie liked Mrs. Cummings. Every day she read a quote from some famous person, in the hope that her students would think about it the rest of the day. This morning, Mrs. Cummings began eloquently as always, every vowel perfectly rounded:

"Roses have thorns, and silver fountains mud;
Clouds are eclipses stain both moon and sun,
And loathsome canker lives in sweetest bud,
All men make faults.

"Shakespeare, Sonnet 33."

She closed her book of quotations and began the lesson. She assigned a book report, due next week, and also wanted each person to find a quote which would sum up the theme of the book.

There was a collective groan from the class. The book report was hard enough, so why the extra work? Frannie herself viewed it as a challenge, but there were many in the class who detested English. Gazing at the back of Gary's head, she wondered how he felt about the assignment. But she knew she wouldn't have the nerve to ask him.

Mrs. Cummings deposited a stack of xeroxed sheets on the first desk of every row to be handed back. The room grew noisy as everyone used the opportunity to turn around and talk. Perspiration grew slimy in Frannie's palms. With the heel of one hand, she nudged her pencil with just enough of a push to send it rolling across the desktop onto the floor. Just as planned, it rolled right under Gary's seat.

With her heart beating fiercely, Frannie waited for Gary to turn around when the papers came, but he didn't. Instead, he flopped the papers over his shoulder, without glancing backward.

He would never know she'd dropped her pencil unless she said something. But she couldn't talk to him!

Shawn McNeil, the boy who sat directly across from Frannie, had seen the pencil drop. "Hey, Gary," he called. "Frannie's pencil is under your desk."

Gary turned around. For one long moment, Frannie was mesmerized by his pale green eyes. "Did you drop your pencil?"

The spell broken, Frannie went red. "Uh, um," she stammered.

He leaned over, his long body half out of the chair, legs splayed in front of him. "Here you go. Next time, say something." He offered the pencil along with a crooked sort of half smile.

She grasped the pencil hard in her slippery hand. "Oh, thank you," she replied a little too enthusiastically, as if he'd just handed her a twenty dollar bill instead of a pencil, causing Mrs. Cummings to give her the evil eye.

"Frances, please be quiet. Now let's go over this sheet together." Gary faced front once more. Frannie's face was burning up.

She wished she could crawl into a hole somewhere, or be somebody else, for it was unbearable being herself.

"I want to quit," Frannie slammed her books down on the lunchroom table and sat down across from Charlene.

"Okay, what happened? Spill it," commanded Charlene, leaning closer.

Frannie was trembling as she tried to unwrap the waxed paper covering her sandwich. "It was awful," she wailed. Val and Patti were shoving their way through the crowd to get to Charlene's and Frannie's table.

"Did we miss anything?" Val asked as she squeezed in next to Frannie.

"No." Frannie took a bite of her bologna sandwich, waiting until the others got settled.

"Did you talk to him?" whispered Patti.

"Yes, a little, but it didn't turn out like you expected at all." She related the whole embarrassing scene, including Mrs. Cummings telling her to be quiet.

"That's a real first. Frannie being scolded for talking," Val declared.

"I said two words, I think," grumbled Frannie. "I just want to quit, now, before I do something really dumb. This is never going to work, not in a million years!"

Charlene reached across the table and grabbed Frannie's wrist. "You're not quitting, do you understand me?" she said in a low, threatening voice. "You got Gary Houseman's attention. He's not going to forget you now. Neither is Shawn McNeil. You may not notice it, but already this plan is working. Give it a chance—I know you'll be glad you did."

That night Frannie wrote in her diary: "*The way Charlene talks, you'd think she's betting her whole life savings on my success with boys. I want to quit this crazy plan so much, but Charlene does have a point—Gary did notice me today, even though I didn't say much.*

"*I don't think I'll be able to go through with the plan tomorrow.*"

Chapter Five

"Here's Page's biology book." Patti thrust the text into Frannie's hands.

"How'd you get it?"

"Oh, I just waited till he took the book out, then tripped him," she explained nonchalantly.

"You did what?" squeaked Frannie in disbelief.

"Yeah, I tripped him. Books flew everywhere. You should've seen him. I helped him pick them up, of course." She grinned mischievously.

"Wow." Frannie pictured poor Page sprawled in the hallway, books scattered all around him. "You're crazy, Patti."

"Now." Patti leaned close to Frannie and whispered conspiratorially, "You read your lines, right?" Frannie nodded. "Okay, get to biology way before Page. When you see him, show him the book and say your lines. Do you remember them?"

"Yes, but I'll probably forget them when I need them," said Frannie. "He doesn't even know me."

"Of course he does. You've had classes together for two years, right? He knows who you are," Patti insisted, pushing her fingers through her short, dark hair.

"I'm not so sure about that."

"Come on, Fran. Stop arguing and get to class."

Patti gave her a friendly shove and sauntered off to her next class.

Frannie's next class was English. As she walked down the aisle to her desk, her eyes locked with Gary Houseman's, and he smiled at her.

Usually, Frannie's face didn't cooperate with her wishes, but this morning, she managed to smile back. Throughout class, she concentrated on Gary's back, hardly hearing Mrs. Cummings at all. He wore a blue-striped T-shirt that emphasized his leanness. Although Frannie didn't know what she could possibly say or do, she wished he would turn around and speak to her. His smile had warmed her all the way to her toes. She found herself noticing things about him that she never paid attention to on people: how light the hairs on his arms were in contrast with his dark skin, how his jeans had been ironed with crisp creases, and the way he lounged in his seat, tapping his pencil absently against his teeth.

When the bell rang, Gary sprang from his seat and bounded out of the classroom, as if he'd just been released from a cage. Slightly disappointed, Frannie took her time gathering up her notebook and purse, forgetting she was supposed to get to biology before Page Garvey. She skimmed into the class just before the second bell rang.

Page, tow-headed and broad shouldered, stood in front of the class, next to their teacher, Mr. Siegle. "Page has lost his biology book. Has anyone seen it?" Mr. Siegle inquired, scanning the room.

Frannie squirmed uncomfortably in her seat. She felt guilty, like a thief, sitting there with

Page's book sandwiched between her own, while everyone in the class said, no, they hadn't seen it. Then the room fell silent.

She *had* to tell him she had it. After all, what would he think if she deliberately held onto the book? He'd surely think she stole it or something, right? She felt the heat in her face as Page's eyes rested upon her, pale blue eyes the color of sea-water. This was the worst moment of her entire life.

Frannie's arm felt leaden as she raised it, painfully aware of what she had to do.

Mr. Siegle nodded to her, "Yes, Frances?"

Page was still looking at her. He had a bony, angular sort of face that was nice-looking in its own way. "Do you want to say something, Frannie?" he urged.

Frannie's reply came out as a strangled whisper. "I—I have your book."

"Hey, great." Page moved toward her. "How'd you get it?"

The rehearsed lines her friends had given had vanished into thin air. Frannie felt totally stupid. She opened her mouth to answer, but nothing came out.

With everyone staring at her, Frannie gave Page his book and hurried past him, out the door.

"Hey, wait!" She heard someone, maybe Page, call after her, but she kept running down the stairs to the girls' restroom.

"Frannie! Oh, Frannie!"

Frannie turned around to see who was calling her just before she opened the door of the first floor restroom. Page ran toward her, his longish hair flying out behind him.

"Hey, wait up, will ya?" He caught up with her finally, breathing hard. "Why'd you run out of there so fast? I just wanted to find out where you found my book and thank you."

Frannie looked up and found his arm gripping her forearm. Her cheeks flooded, for, at the same time that she was experiencing terrific embarrassment, she realized she enjoyed his touch. "I found it in the main hall." The lines came back to her. Page's locker was near the attendance office. "By the attendance office," she added.

He grinned. He was not so much tall as broad, Frannie noted. What Charlene would call a "football physique."

"Well, thanks a lot," he said. "I really appreciate it." He let go of her arm.

"You're welcome," she managed, wondering what to do next. With Page standing here next to her, she hardly could escape into the restroom now.

"We'd better get back to class," he suggested. His palm touched her elbow, and she felt a small thrill travel up her arm. "That is," he put in, "unless you're still running away."

Frannie giggled. Page winked at her knowingly, as if he wanted to reassure her everything was okay. Easily, Frannie replied, "No, let's go to class now."

As they entered the biology room, Frannie braced herself for all those inquiring eyes. It was slightly better coming in with Page, but still her shyness enveloped her like a gunnysack the minute she stepped through the doorway.

As she expected, there were the usual snickers and knowing glances that were always generated when a boy and a girl entered the room together (especially when everyone was unaccustomed to seeing them together). Page took it all in good humor. It must come naturally to him, thought Frannie, whose own smile was a pasted-on shield against teasing comments.

"A popular person can do just about anything and get away with it, but an unpopular one has to work hard not to do anything too weird or she can become the butt of a joke," Frannie scribbled in her diary later. *"Everyone looked at me like I was weird, and I felt like a real jerk. But Page was really cool about it. He was very nice to me, too, and made me feel a lot better about the whole dumb thing."*

Charlene came over that evening with her make-up kit to give Frannie a makeup lesson.

"So far so good, Fran," Charlene said, dabbing blobs of clear face makeup on Frannie's nose, cheeks, chin and forehead. "I don't care what you think of this plan, but it's working. You're definitely getting noticed. In a way it's like a publicity campaign, like they do with celebrities."

"Ugh!" commented Frannie.

"Come on, hold still!" Charlene commanded as she smoothed the makeup evenly over Frannie's skin. "Maybe you should get on the school paper or something. Maybe even try out for cheerleading."

"I don't write too well—and you know I hate sports."

"Still, you've got lots of talents no one at school

except Patti, Val and me know about." Charlene brushed on a pink-toned blusher. "Anyway, it doesn't matter. Pretty soon you'll be totally un-forgettable." She ordered Frannie to hold still while she applied a coat of lip gloss. "There, have a look. Amazing, isn't it?"

Frannie faced the mirror. She looked different, really pretty. Charlene was a genius with makeup—much better than her own clumsy attempts.

The blue shadow picked out the color in Frannie's eyes, while a soft brown pencil, used to outline them, made them stand out. The blusher Charlene used brought out the color in her cheeks without making them appear too rosy.

"You'll have to teach me how to do all of this," Frannie told her eagerly. Making up your face was an art in itself, she realized, a little like mixing paints—finding the right colors to go with your skin tone and hair color. You would no more throw makeup on a face than you would throw paint onto a canvas.

"All I did was shade a highlight that's already there," was how Charlene put it.

After Charlene left, Frannie stood back from the mirror to study herself. Her mother also came in to view the finished product.

"Frannie, you look fantastic," she raved, squeez-ing her daughter's shoulders. "As much as I hate to admit it, it's about time for you to get your own supplies, I can see that."

In spite of her mixed feelings about her day, Frannie couldn't help but be excited about her new appearance. *"I didn't know I could look this pretty,"* she confided to her diary.

Chapter Six

Frannie didn't run into Fred Brown at the lockers until just before fifth period art. As she was walking down the hall, she caught sight of Ronnie Schell at the end of the corridor slamming his locker door, a stack of poster boards under one arm. All her attention zeroed in on him. With kids jostling past her, she stopped at her own locker and simply stared. Then Fred, whose locker was directly below hers, bolted up and knocked her books right out of her arms.

Frannie couldn't have made them scatter more if she'd wanted to—which, she remembered, was the whole idea. The look on Fred's face was one of pure embarrassment. "Oh, Frances, I'm sorry. Excuse me!"

Propping his glasses nervously, Fred dropped to his knees and scooped up the books. Frannie knelt beside him.

"Really, it's okay, Freddie. It wasn't your fault," she said, surprised at herself for not being nervous. She didn't have to clear her throat once.

"I'm really a klutz, Frances," he went on. "I should have looked where I was going." He smiled self-consciously, the dimples in his cheeks deepening, as he handed her a pile of books.

"Thanks, Freddie, I appreciate your help."

"What do you have next?" Fred arranged his own books under one arm. Frannie noticed how thin and freckled his arms were, sticking out at bony angles from the striped knit shirt he wore.

"Art," she replied. "Mr. Carniglia."

"Oh, good. I've got gym. I'll walk you there." He waited while she shoved two books in her locker and cradled the rest of them in the crook of her arm.

Frannie was amazed at how easy the conversation went. They talked about their classes. She learned that Freddie was very interested in science and that he planned on majoring in physics in college. Frannie didn't really know too much about physics but she didn't dare ask him about it. Her knowledge was limited to high school biology and general science. Freddie went on to say that he wasn't exactly sure what he wanted to do for the rest of his life. Frannie wasn't sure, either, but she voiced her thoughts.

Before she knew it they had reached Frannie's classroom. "Nice talking to you, Freddie," she said.

Freddie's smile was broad. "Same here, Frances. Thanks for not being mad. See you."

As she stepped into the art room, she thought about what had just happened. For the first time in her life, a boy had walked her to class. Of course, Fred Brown was just about the friendliest boy in school, and he did all the talking about what he wanted to talk about, but still . . .

She looked around for Ronnie, but he wasn't

there. Remembering the poster board he was carrying earlier, she figured he was doing some kind of special assignment.

Adam Stone was engaged in a lively conversation with two popular girls, Lucy Marshall and Jo Curry. Frannie wondered if he was a good choice for Thursday. Would he ever bother to speak to her? He was so good-looking.

On Thursday, Frannie entered that same classroom filled with nervous anticipation. She fidgeted through the first ten minutes of class, wondering how she would get to talk to Adam. The day before, after the quiz, the class had sketched a still life of an apple, orange and bananas in a cheap gold bowl. Today they would do a watercolor of the same thing.

Ronnie Schell sauntered in for a few minutes to talk to Mr. Carniglia, then left. This assignment was probably too elementary for him, thought Frannie.

When it was time to get the paints, Frannie tried to get in line behind Adam, but Lucy Marshall wove her way between them.

"Lucy, my love, how are you?" Adam greeted her, and Frannie could tell by his silky tone that the two shared a fondness for each other. He always spoke intimately to girls he dated, as if each one were the most important person on earth.

I wish someone would talk to me like that, dreamed Frannie.

Adam selected a fine sable brush and painted a silver dot of tempera on the end of Lucy's cutely turned-up nose. Her delighted giggle rose above the students' chatter, and everyone turned to stare at the pair.

Frannie shuffled along next to them, listening to their conversation while outwardly pretending they didn't interest her in the least.

"Blue. Let's try blue," Adam suggested, dipping his brush in the color.

"No, yellow." Lucy laughed. Mr. Carniglia made a motion for Lucy to quiet down. Obediently, she located her paint box and took her seat. Quickly, Adam followed suit.

Frannie sat down and immersed herself in her painting. Watercolors were hard to get just right, but the fruit came to life under the skill of her brushwork. While she was working, Mr. Carniglia passed out the graded test papers.

Now, if she just had the opportunity to stand next to Adam, she could ask him how he did on the test, instead of how he *thought* he did on the test. Frannie's throat constricted with fear at the thought of speaking to him, though.

At cleanup time, Frannie was one of the first to reach the sink. She was yanking the rough paper towels out of the dispenser to dry her hands when Adam and Lucy sauntered up, side by side. They were laughing quietly, obviously sharing some secret joke.

"So you didn't get to talk to him?" Val inquired later.

"There was no way. Lucy had his undivided attention," explained Frannie, while peering in the mirror at her tonsils. "I think I have a sore throat."

"It's just psychological," Charlene said. She bit down noisily on a potato chip.

The four girls were gathered in Frannie's bedroom for another conference, huddled around a spread of potato chips, dip and soft drinks.

"Have a Coke, Frannie. I think it's just nerves," Val offered. "I bet you got yourself all worked up about talking to Adam, right?"

"He was pretty scary," she admitted. "Anyway, I bet if I was able to ask him something, I would've blown it."

"Don't talk like that. Look what you've done so far." Patti ran her fingers through her feathered hair. "You've had Page Garvey running to your rescue, Fred Brown walking you to class and Gary Houseman paying attention to you. You can always try Adam some other time. Watch, next week he'll probably be interested in someone else."

"I've got an idea for the Halloween dance for Frannie," Charlene interjected. She beamed with such bright intensity, it made Frannie wonder what she had up her sleeve this time.

"You know I can't dance! You're not going to put me through that again, Charlene!" she wailed in despair.

Charlene's voice grew conspiratorially low. "This time it's gonna be different, completely different. Don't worry about the dancing. We'll teach you how to dance, and you'll do just fine. The way I see it, we'll rent you a costume—a special costume of a romantic heroine. Somebody like . . ." She pretended to think. ". . . Scarlet O'Hara or one of those ladies from a historical romance."

"So? What's that going to do for me?" Frannie was skeptical.

Val squeezed her hand. "Frannie, don't you see? Charlene's right. We'll dress you up and make you look so fantastic nobody will be able to ignore you. Everybody'll be asking, 'Who is this mystery woman?' "

"Then they'll know—it's Frances Bronson. You know, that shy, bookish girl in school," added Charlene.

Frannie laughed. "So what's gonna make me so special? I'll bet there'll be plenty of other cute girls with great costumes."

"But yours will be spectacular," Charlene hurried on. "And you'll make a grand entrance, of course. We'll choose just the right moment for you to appear on the scene."

"Yeah, just before the music starts," suggested Val. "And then she'll appear . . . and a hush will fall over the room." Val glided across the bedroom, lost in her own theatrics.

The girls laughed. "You're crazy!" cried Frannie, enjoying herself thoroughly.

"Dance lessons begin this weekend!" Patti announced. "Now let's get serious and talk about the football game tomorrow night. Char, I guess you'll be going out with Jason afterwards, huh?"

Charlene nodded mistily. Frannie's friend had been on cloud nine since the dance last week. Frannie was always amazed by Charlene, for when she set her sights on a boy, she usually got him. How lucky she was!

Patti turned to Valerie. "Are you going?"

"I might not go if Bert's still got the flu," she explained. "Otherwise, maybe we could double?"

"Sure," replied Patti. "If he's still sick, though, maybe you could go with Fran. She could use the exposure."

"Uh, no thanks. I don't like football."

"Why not? We could sit with Charlene. She's gonna be alone until the game's over," urged Val.

"I don't think so," Frannie repeated.

"Well, whatever you decide, Scott and I will be snuggled together up in those bleachers," Patti said, fiercely batting her eyelashes.

Patti and her boyfriend Scott were one of those couples that belonged together naturally. Most boys were much shorter than Patti, who at five foot eight was a little self-conscious about her height. But Scott, at six foot two, towered over her—and she loved it.

Once more, Frannie wished there were someone special for her. Her friends never made her feel left out on purpose, but often, like right now, she felt like she was the odd girl out. Even though she liked listening and imagining herself in their place, it was no substitute for having her own dates and her own plans. She caught herself envying her friends for those close times they shared with their special guys, fogging up the windows of his car, enveloped in their own private world of love . . .

But dreaming herself into her friends' situations was not satisfying her anymore. She wanted her own experience. She wanted someone to call her own boyfriend, someone she could always count on for Friday and Saturday night dates, someone to share her thoughts and dreams with. The longing had grown into a dull, but very persistent ache in her heart, which Frannie divulged to no one, except to her diary, where her deepest worry blossomed into the words: *"Will I ever have a special boyfriend?"*

Chapter Seven

To Frannie's relief, no part of the plan took place during school hours on Friday. The whole school was buzzing with the characteristic "thank goodness it's Friday" excitement, plus the usual anticipation over the game. Though it was of little concern to her, Lincoln's team was playing a stiff contender, one of their arch rivals. To the girls, who was going with whom was at least as important (if not more) than who was playing whom.

Emmett Caldwell sat directly across from Frannie in biology. He was a beanpole of a boy with a mass of freckles that nearly covered him from head to toe. Even his lips had freckles, Frannie noticed. He wore his hair really short, much shorter than most boys on campus, about which she'd heard his friends tease him. To her advantage he was about the smartest person in this class, a good person to ask about a homework assignment. Besides, he would never guess she was calling for any other reason than biology.

During class, Emmett didn't look Frannie's way once, which was fine with her. Knowing that she would be calling him tonight made her nervous. After all, she'd never phoned a boy before.

Ronnie Schell had set up an easel in the art room right under the skylight. It was also next to the sink, which meant Frannie couldn't help but pass him and notice his work.

As she stood waiting her turn to use the sink, Ronnie must have sensed her watching him. "Like it?" he inquired shyly, half-turning in his seat.

She was mesmerized by the way his brush-strokes caught the essence of movement in the dancing figures. A boy dressed like Paul Revere and a girl in a long, hooped gown of the same period dominated the foreground. Behind the couple was a muted scene of children bobbing for apples. A poster for the Halloween dance, she assumed.

Propped against the built-in storage cabinet was yet another poster of a dancing couple dressed as the wolf and Little Red Riding Hood.

But Frannie loved the first picture best. With what appeared to be complete ease, Ronnie added a line of ripply lace to the bodice of the girl's dress.

"Oh, I like it a lot," Frannie breathed, forgetting herself entirely. The Paul Revere couple was so full of life she could see them twirling right off the poster board.

"They're for the Halloween dance, aren't they, Ron?" Mark Fromm, who was standing behind Frannie, asked.

"Yep. I'm going to put them up this afternoon," Ronnie said. "That is if I get the lettering done in time."

Frannie thought it was a shame to put lettering on such beautiful pictures, but she didn't say anything, for she knew even Ronnie's lettering would be beautiful.

She would like to have stood and watched him paint all afternoon. As it was, she realized those few moments had pleased her so much that her thoughts returned to Ronnie at his easel again and again that day, and even long after that. Now this is a boy I'd like to date, she thought wistfully.

At three-thirty the halls teemed with restless activity. Lockers slammed shut on the school week, kids shouted down the halls to their friends, while others clustered outside on the front walk of the school.

Frannie met Charlene and Jason at their lockers. "Well, how'd it go today?" her friend wanted to know.

"Okay."

"One more tonight," Charlene winked at her. "Good luck." She stood close to Jason, who relieved her of an armload of books.

"Have fun tonight," Frannie wished them both. Jason smiled warmly at her.

"Don't worry, we will," he answered, and Frannie thought, that's one more boy I've talked to, even if he's attached!

The house was empty when Frannie got home. Out of habit she poured herself a glass of milk and plucked an apple from the fruit basket, then settled in front of the TV in her room. It would be two hours until her mother arrived home, and shortly after that, her father. With that in mind, she figured now would be the best time to call Emmett.

Frannie wanted to stall for time, though. The assignment had been to read pages 220–230 for Monday and answer the ten questions at the end of the chapter. Assignments in that class varied very little, so she'd have to be careful not to appear stupid, especially to someone as bright as Emmett. Finally, after some fifteen minutes of deliberating, she mustered her courage, looked up Emmett's number and dialed.

It rang and rang. No answer. She breathed a sigh of relief. She could scratch him off the list entirely, and tell the girls Emmett wasn't home. It would be easy enough to do, unless they'd make her keep trying, just as they planned to do with Adam Stone. Might as well try him later and get it over with, she concluded.

While she was waiting for someone to come home at the Caldwell residence, Frannie browsed through her diary. The last four days had brought some results, she had to admit. She'd had conversations with four different boys. Five, if you included Jason. Before the plan, Frannie had gone for months without any contact with boys— even the "hi" or "pass the papers, please" variety.

Now, in spite of all her protests about the plan, she could see from the daily record of events that her life was changing from dull to somewhat interesting.

She dialed again at five o'clock. This time Emmett answered on the first ring. "Hello?"

"Hi. Is this Emmett?" She cleared her throat self-consciously.

"Yes. Who's this?" At least he sounded friendly, she thought, relieved.

"This is Frances Bronson. I—I sit across from you in biology." She explained her position in relation to him, just in case he'd never noticed her there.

"Oh, hi, Frances." He knew who she was, and he cleared his throat, too. Frannie was glad she wasn't the only one who did that. "What's up?"

"I lost the biology assignment for the weekend. I figured you'd have it," she said, glancing at her written script.

"Oh, yeah. Just a sec. Lemme go get it . . ."

Footsteps receded away from the phone. She heard a shuffling of papers, a snatch of conversation, probably with his mother or brother or sister. Then he was on the phone once more, reading off the assignment which Frannie had written in her notebook in front of her. "Oh, thanks, Emmett. Thanks a lot," she told him, smiling into the receiver, even though he couldn't see her face.

"Oh, sure," he replied, obviously slightly overwhelmed by all those thank you's. "Is that all?"

"Yes." Frannie stopped herself from saying "thank you" again. Yet the following pause was an uncomfortable one in which she searched for something to say to wrap up the conversation (there were no lines to memorize for that). "Ha—have a nice weekend," she finally said.

"You too. Bye," he said and then hung up.

Frannie replaced the receiver. Her heart pounded, loudly it seemed, in the silent room. She did it! She had called a boy on the telephone, actually *called* a boy. Of course, this event would not hit the front page of a big city newspaper, and it was maybe not as big a deal as climbing Mount Everest, but nonetheless, she had done it. A major breakthrough. She felt great.

Chapter Eight

"Sempel's having a special on cosmetics today," Mrs. Bronson told Frannie at breakfast on Saturday. "And makeup demonstrations, too. Want to go?"

"Sure," answered Frannie eagerly, amazed at her mother's interest. Until this week she had discouraged Frannie from wearing more than a little blusher, claiming she was too young to be putting lots of "junk" on her face. "You really mean it?"

"You're growing up, Fran," Mrs. Bronson answered. "I promised you when the time came I'd let you use makeup. Maybe we'll get you some new clothes, too. Make a shopping day of it," her mother decided.

"Sounds good."

"Frannie's beautiful just as she is, Joan," her father protested. "She doesn't need any makeup."

Joan Bronson laughed. "We're not going to rebuild her, Sam, only enhance her beauty," she reassured her husband.

"Let's hope so," giggled Frannie.

"Just come home with the same Frannie. I don't like surprises." Mr. Bronson wagged a warning finger at them both.

"Don't worry, Dad. Mom's not going to let them make me into a wanton woman. I don't change that easily," she told him, but even as she said it, she wondered about herself. The plan already had changed her a little, but she doubted if anyone, least of all her parents, noticed it. And that even if they could, she realized they would catalogue it under that broad heading known to parents as "growing up."

Just last night Frannie's mother and father had attributed her retreat to her room to watch TV as part of growing up. What Frannie really did, however, was drift from one daydream to another, imagining for a few moments Ronnie Schell in a picture postcard scene, quietly painting at his easel outside a sidewalk cafe in Paris, or Ronnie at a showing of his artwork in San Francisco. The one she liked best was of him studying her with the same careful absorption he gave to his paintings.

Repeatedly, Frannie had tried to construct the feeling she got from standing behind Ronnie, watching him, but she'd got only the flavor of it. Still, that had been enough. She'd pretended that time stood still, that a circle was drawn around them, shutting out the rest of the class and that all she could feel or hear was the painting sound of his brushstrokes, Ronnie's quiet voice and the intent look on his face. She'd let herself get absorbed in the daydream for hours.

The mall was crowded with hordes of Saturday shoppers. Caught in the press of people, Frannie and her mother nearly lost each other twice. At

Sempel's they grabbed the first empty seats they saw in the cosmetics department.

"Hi, Maxine," Joan Bronson waved to the red-headed saleswoman in that department.

"Can't stay away, even on your day off, huh?" Maxine called out. Her hair was that stiff, overly dyed kind, Frannie noted upon closer inspection, and she wore heavy makeup. Frannie hoped she wouldn't use that much on her.

"No. Sempel's is like a magnet—it keeps drawing me here," Mrs. Bronson laughed gaily.

Frannie loved the way her mother talked with people. She made it look easy, as if it were second nature to her.

"My daughter wants a new look, or rather"—she winked at Frannie—"an enhanced look."

Maxine eyed Frannie with obvious approval. "Well, that shouldn't be too difficult. You've got a lot to start with. Frances, isn't it?"

"Everyone calls me Frannie," she corrected.

Maxine stood back and studied Frannie's complexion carefully, then selected what she thought would be the proper colors. A light, clear foundation, rosy blush, white creme for under the eyes and a shadow stick for her cheeks. "To accentuate the cheekbones," Maxine explained.

Then the eyes. Brown and blue shadow, a soft brown eye crayon, like Charlene had used for outlining, and mascara. Maxine explained every step of the procedure so Frannie would know how to recreate the look herself. When it was all done, Frannie leaned forward to examine her reflection in the mirror.

She needn't have worried about Maxine using

too much makeup—it looked absolutely perfect. Even Charlene could probably learn a thing or two from this woman, thought Frannie.

"You look very pretty," her mother commented. "Not too much—just right."

Maxine was tweezing her eyebrows now, shaping them. "Frannie, you look stunning, really. Your skin is so flawless." With a lip brush, she applied a glossy peach lipstick.

"Thanks so much, Maxine," Frannie told her gratefully, rising from the chair. "I love it."

Maxine let out a hearty laugh, oblivious to the women who were crowding in, anxious to take Frannie's empty seat. "I'm glad—you should love your face. That's what I'm here for, to make people love their faces!"

Joan Bronson bought Frannie most of the makeup she was wearing. Afterward, they went upstairs to the junior department. Joan said hello to everyone, for she knew every employee in the whole department store.

"Let's get something to go with that sweater," she suggested, tugging at the sleeve of the blue pullover Frannie was wearing. They located a rack of plaid skirts on sale, and flipped through them until they found a match.

By lunchtime, Frannie had bought a new blue plaid skirt, a silky peach blouse, jeans and of course, the makeup. They stopped for hamburgers, then bundled up their purchases and drove home. "I'm so pleased with everything, Mom." Frannie couldn't keep from smiling, imagining how she would look in her new clothes.

"You'll be a real hit, Fran."

Frannie nearly laughed aloud. Me, a hit? Frances Bronson, that shy bug everyone was trying to pry out of the closet? How different she felt!

Frannie was in her room trying on her new clothes, when the phone rang. She secretly hoped it was one of her friends who wanted to go to a movie or something, but that rarely happened anymore. Val, Patti and Charlene were nearly always tied up with their boyfriends.

"Frannie! Phone!"

"Coming!"

"Hi, it's me, Charlene. Where've you been?" she asked. "We've been trying to get a hold of you all day!"

"Mom took me shopping. We got some fabulous makeup, and clothes—" Frannie brimmed with news, but Charlene cut her off.

"Listen, what about the dance lessons? We've got only an hour and a half to spare before we have to get ready for tonight. We'll be right over."

Panic fluttered in Frannie's heart. Dances and parties were terrifying to her. Didn't Charlene realize that? As much as she felt she'd changed in the past week, she certainly hadn't changed enough to handle a dance without panicking.

In spite of her diffidence, Frannie got her first dance lesson that afternoon.

"Don't worry," Val assured her. "By next Saturday, we'll make sure you won't step on anyone's toes."

"As long as she discos, she won't have to worry about anybody's toes," Patti commented.

Frannie felt the dance steps were awkward and

she felt extremely silly doing them. "I feel like a robot," she giggled.

"Just practice every day and you'll lighten up." Charlene demonstrated, but her hip swivels and hand motions seemed so graceful in comparison with Frannie's.

Suddenly Frannie threw up her hands in despair. "I'll never be able to do this right!"

"Oh, yes, you will," argued Charlene. "Where's your faith, girl. Besides, none of the guys at school are John Travolta. Nobody's gonna expect you to do anything too wild."

Frannie's father stood in the doorway of the living room, watching the girls. "May I have this dance?" he asked Frannie. He took her and twirled her round and round the coffee table.

The other girls collapsed with laughter. "Mr. Bronson, you're a great dancer, but so old-fashioned!"

He pretended to look surprised. "Oh? And I thought I was with it! A simple waltz never goes out of fashion, does it?"

Frannie blushed not so much because of what her father said, but because the word "old-fashioned" reminded her of the picture of the girl in the Revolutionary War dress. At that moment, she knew exactly what she wanted to wear to the Halloween dance.

Grinning at her own private joke, Frannie asked them all, "Can anyone here teach me the minuet?"

The four of them burst into new laughter, as she knew they would.

"Even if we could, Fran, who's going to dance it with you?" Val teased.

Ronnie, thought Frannie. She imagined the two of them, like the Paul Revere couple in the picture, sweeping together across a marble floor with perfect timing, with the reflections from a twinkling chandelier lighting up their faces.

Chapter Nine

On Monday, the plan called for Frannie to buy a candy bar at lunch and offer it to Ernie Sanchez in history class. Ernie sat in front of her, and every day just before the second bell rang, he'd yell out, "Anybody got anything to eat?" Why he didn't just bring an extra large lunch, Frannie didn't know.

Consequently nicknamed "Jaws" by his classmates, Ernie was one of Lincoln's biggest and most feared football players. When Ernie fell on you, his teammates joked, you felt like you'd been flattened by a ton of bricks. In class, he resembled a huge bear stuffed into his inadequate desk with hands like giant paws curled around a pencil.

Anyway, the girls had chosen him for the plan because of his appetite and his penchant for Hershey bars, which of course was what Frannie bought.

Ernie was not what you'd call fat, Frannie considered as she watched him swagger through the door, he was a wall of solid muscle. The flat plane of his face broke into a wide grin when he bellowed, as if on cue, "Hey, anyone got anything to eat in here?"

Frannie had her lines memorized. "I have a

Hershey bar," she offered shyly, happily surprised that her voice didn't flee her.

"I'll take it." Ernie sprinted toward her, slammed his books down on his desk and relieved her of the candy bar. "Thanks. You're a lifesaver, Frances." He winked, which made her blush, then squeezed himself into his desk. Score another one for Frannie.

After school, Frannie and Charlene went to a costume shop to select their Halloween outfits. Charlene decided on a bumblebee costume, but Frannie wasn't satisfied with anything she saw.

"What about the Southern Belle dress? That would look great on you," Charlene urged.

"It's not what I've got in mind." Then an idea popped into her head. "I think I'll make my costume," she announced to her friend. She was an excellent seamstress, and the dress she had in mind couldn't be that hard to make. If she needed help, Frannie was sure her mother would give her a hand.

At a fabric store, she purchased a pattern for eighteenth and nineteenth century dresses, which allowed her to create a number of styles just by changing the fabric of a collar or sleeve.

Tuesday after school Frannie phoned Gary Houseman for the English homework. "I lost the assignment," she said, giving him the rehearsed little white lie.

"Oh, sure, Frannie. I'll get it." She heard him thumbing through his binder before he located it and read it off to her.

"Thanks, Gary," she told him appreciatively. Talking to boys *was* getting easier.

"How'd you do on the last test?" he asked, just as she was thinking of a graceful way to hang up.

"Uh, an A." It was her usual grade, but she felt embarrassed. What if Gary got a lesser grade—would he feel bad?

"You topped me. I got a B!" he said.

"Well, that's still good," Frannie blurted out too quickly.

"Yeah. Some days are better than others," he answered casually. There was a long pause, in which Frannie tried to think of something to say, but nothing came to her.

"Can I do anything else for you?" he asked.

"Oh, no thanks. The assignment is all," she replied in an embarrassed rush, as an uninvited picture of his hair curling gently over his collar filled her mind.

"Well, okay. See you in class tomorrow, then?" He posed it as a question.

"Sure, and thanks again. Bye."

After she replaced the receiver, her hands flew to her face. How flushed she was! It was a good thing Gary couldn't see her now, she thought as she put on her coat.

Outside, the brisk autumn air assaulted her burning skin and made it tingle. Frannie hopped on a bus to Sempel's, where she was to meet her mother to go shopping for fabric.

She could see that twice was all she could use the plan on any one boy. If she tried it more often than that, there was the danger that he would think she had a mad crush on him, and that could be horribly embarrassing. Already, Gary might think so, from their conversation this afternoon, plus the pencil scene of last week. Frannie decided to make a point not to cross his path at school or approach him again, just in case he was suspicious.

Joan Bronson was in Sempel's display window, helping the window dresser with the unobliging head of a mannequin, when Frannie arrived.

"Saved by my daughter," she exclaimed, tossing the head to the assistant behind her. "I'll leave this up to you."

Frannie followed her mother to the fabrics department, where they spent an exhaustive half hour going through aisles of materials before finally settling on a pale, robin's egg blue sateen. So many yards of material were necessary to make the dress that Frannie had to watch the cost.

"After all, how many opportunities are you going to have to wear this dress again, Fran?" her mother reasoned, propelling her quickly out of the expensive satins into the cheaper, cotton-based fabrics.

Several yards of creamy lace for the bodice and sleeves, some pearly little buttons, thread and a zipper completed the purchase. Frannie was thrilled. The dress would be a masterpiece. She couldn't wait to get started.

On Wednesday, Frannie was to borrow a pencil from Page Garvey during biology. She was dead tired, as her friends had kept her up with their persistent dancing lessons until way past her regular bedtime. Not only had she forgotten to bring her lines to memorize, she hadn't even looked at them.

Fortunately, the class was dissecting frogs in the lab, so Frannie found it quite easy to maneuver herself beside Page. Nervously she cleared her throat, at the same time wishing she wouldn't do that.

Page looked at her and smiled warmly. "Hi, bookfinder," he greeted her.

Frannie wished she could control the blush that pricked her skin at all the wrong moments. Taking a deep breath, she asked, "Can I borrow a pencil?"

"Sure," he grinned. "I bet you're going to write all this down." He cocked his head in the direction of Mr. Siegle, who was explaining something to the class.

She giggled, then clamped a hand over her mouth to suppress it. "I'll try. Thanks," she said, accepting Page's stubby pencil. She moved closer to the lab table.

"Hey," Page called to her, but Mr. Siegle interrupted him.

"Page, please pay attention. Conversation can wait, unless you want to share it with the whole class."

A few students snickered. Frannie pretended to take enormous interest in the dissected frog, hoping the snickers weren't meant for her. She prayed this incident wouldn't revive last week's running out of the classroom scene in the other students' minds. And if it didn't, she prayed even harder that no one would mention it now.

The moment passed without incident and everyone settled back to work. Frannie broke out in a cold sweat. It wasn't until after class was dismissed that she began to wonder what Page had been about to say to her.

Despite Charlene, Patti and Val's teasing probes for information over lunch, Frannie managed to keep that little morsel to herself, telling them only about the brief pencil conversation.

"Sounds like you're making real progress," Patti wagged her head in amazement. "And to think you did this one without lines!"

Frannie smiled secretively. The topic switched to the upcoming Halloween dance and what costumes Patti and Val should wear.

For the past two days, Ronnie Schell had been in and out of art class, working on a project for Mr. Carniglia. Frannie found herself watching the door, hoping to catch a glimpse of him. On Wednesday, Ronnie walked in quietly, as if he didn't want anyone to notice him. By the time Frannie saw him, he stood next to Mr. Carniglia near the cupboards, where they were discussing some drawings.

Frannie stole a glance in their direction. Ronnie smiled at something Mr. Carniglia said, then his eyes met Frannie's. Was it her imagination, or did the corners of his mouth turn up slightly in a smile meant just for her?

No, it couldn't be, she told herself. The difference in his expression was too slight, to insignificant, and it might not have existed at all. Her eyes must have been playing tricks on her.

She looked away, listening to the rise and fall of his voice, until he left the room.

The rest of the afternoon went uneventfully, until after sixth period.

It was Frannie's habit to hurry from her last period class to her locker before the crowd. Today she breezed out, not looking to either side of her, intent on getting to that locker.

"Frannie?"

She whirled around in surprise at the sound of a boy's voice calling her name. It was Page. Slowly he approached her. "Frannie, can we talk?"

"Uh, sure," she replied uncertainly. In a daze, she let him lead her away from the bustle of kids emerging from the classrooms.

"Do you want to go to the game this week?" he ventured, shifting from one foot to the other.

Frannie was taken completely off guard. Stuttering, she asked: "W-with you?"

"Yeah, who else? The boogey man?" He grinned, his ears went pink, and he glanced down at his jogging shoes.

She stifled a giggle. "Oh, sure. Uh, that would be nice."

He nodded. "Great. I'll pick you up about seven, Friday night, okay?"

Frannie didn't remember her mouth forming the word "yes," though she guessed she must have said it. In a state of total shock, she floated to her locker and even managed to dig out the right books to take home.

For the first time in her life, Frances Bronson was going on a date!

Chapter Ten

"You got a date? Super!" Charlene squeezed Frannie's cold fingers in between her own. "Aren't you excited?"

"More nervous than excited," admitted Frannie, for now the reality of spending an entire evening with a boy she hardly knew started to bear down on her. It scared her to death.

A cloud scudded in front of the sun, turning Charlene's room a shade darker. It was a spacious room—a garage turned into a rumpus room and now a bedroom—opened up on one side by a long sliding glass door onto the patio. Frannie had helped decorate it, selecting the pink and green plaid curtains, matching spread and celery-green carpeting.

"Well, you can't walk around forever with that ridiculous look on your face, but it'll do for now. Do you know anything about football?" Charlene suddenly closed her eyes as though in pain. "Oh, no; don't tell me. I know."

Frannie knew Charlene was remembering the two games she'd dragged her to, when she had cheered in all the wrong places, and even rooted for the other team.

"You'll have to learn," Charlene said abruptly.

"What?"

"I said you'll have to learn something about football before Friday night. You don't want to look stupid, do you?"

Frannie shivered. The last thing she wanted to do was look stupid. "I just won't cheer then," she said.

Charlene leaned closer, as if revealing a rare confidence. "Look, Fran, Page is a big football fan. He won't want to sit there knowing you're bored to death. You accepted his invitation, now you have to fit in at least a little."

"So between now and Friday I'm supposed to become a football fan? Don't I have enough to do, with the dance lessons, the dress I'm making, the plan . . . ?"

"All you have to do is memorize a few plays. Look at some books during study period tomorrow." Frannie groaned and made a face at the word "memorize." "You want this date to be a success, don't you?" Charlene persisted.

"Yes, but I never thought it would be this much trouble."

"I brushed up a little myself when I started dating Jason," Charlene noted.

That night, exhausted, Frannie crawled into bed and opened her diary, which she'd neglected for a couple of days. *"Dear Diary, I'm sorry I've neglected you, but instead of having nothing to write about, I've had too much to say, and too much to do."*

She went on to describe the wonderful dress she and her mother were making, the dance lessons that she was beginning to enjoy and the date she would be having on Friday.

"Sometimes I feel like it's getting easier to talk to boys, like my friends said it would. And other times I still get really scared and don't know what to say, like the other day when I was talking to Gary on the phone. And I'm so afraid of people laughing at me.

"I hope the date goes okay. What are we going to talk about all night?"

Poring over several books in the school library the next day, Frannie decided that learning football was like doing homework, or memorizing for a test. A hard test. She didn't even know the positions, let alone plays, so she was starting in on the ground floor. Charlene was crazy if she thought she could learn so much in two days!

At least all her activity kept Frannie from having time to be nervous about the plan. Later that day, almost like an old pro, she dropped her pencil so that it rolled under Emmett Caldwell's desk. He retrieved it for her, she said "thank you" and everything went smoothly.

On Friday she had to ask Chuck Stanley, who sat behind her in algebra, a question relating to what the teacher was talking about. A sleek-haired, cocky sort of boy, Chuck was a casual-to-not-very-good student, whom Frannie had little reason to talk to before.

Her opportunity came when Mr. Randall passed back a problem sheet, which he usually did on Fridays. Before the handouts reached her, she glanced at her "lines to memorize" tucked inside her binder.

As she handed the sheets to Chuck, she asked, "Do we do these in class or at home?"

Chuck was sprawled in his chair as he usually was, looking too lazy to sit up. His sharp brown eyes appraised her mockingly. "Since when do you ask me anything, girl? You're the smart one," he teased.

Embarrassment welled up inside her and registered on her face. She couldn't think of any good comeback, so she whirled around to face the front. Behind Frannie, Chuck rustled papers. "Just kidding," he said, stifling a laugh. "It's homework."

Frannie's "thank you" came out stiff, forced. How in the world could she handle conversation on a date, when she had trouble even saying thank you?

Spotlights blazed long, swirling beams through the darkness, illuminating the expanse of the football field. Emanating from the loudspeaker was a garbled message that Frannie couldn't understand. Whatever it was about, the crowd clapped and cheered.

"Let's not miss the kickoff," Page hurried Frannie through the gate and pulled her by the hand up the bleachers.

Frannie needn't have worried about making conversation with Page, for he had carried it single-handedly from the moment they'd left her house. Her parents had behaved themselves, too, not asking too many questions about what Page's father did for a living and what kind of car he drove.

All Page talked about on the way to the game was football, which required only minimal responses from Frannie. She quickly realized that her crash course in football did not even dent this boy's knowledge of the subject, but she was still relieved to have learned a few pieces of terminology, thanks to Charlene.

The loudspeaker squawked loudly and the cheerleaders bounded up and down as the home team jogged onto the field.

"Here we go, Lincoln!" Page's blue eyes were fixed on the field. Momentarily, Frannie wondered why he had even asked her to come!

The crowd roared and cheered, and Frannie watched the cheerleaders to make sure she didn't make the same mistakes with her cheering as she had before.

Out on the field, the players took their positions. "Lincoln has a balanced line," Frannie said, hoping she was correct.

Page glanced at her with mild surprise, then quickly turned his attention back to the field, terrified of missing anything.

The ball soared into the air. The blue and gold jersey-clad receiver caught the ball, and cradling it in his arms, rocketed forward, colliding with two players from the opposition who tumbled him to the ground.

The referee's whistle blew shrilly. Frannie searched her new vocabulary for something appropriate to say and came up with "a good power play."

Page was on his feet, but when he heard Frannie he spun around to stare at her before the players broke their huddle.

"Lincoln, Lincoln—yeah!" the cheerleaders chorused, plumes of steam rising from their efforts. "Hold that line, hold that line!"

"Second down," Frannie piped.

Page dropped onto the bleacher beside her. "You sure know your football," he said.

She flushed pink. "Well, I've read some books."

"Oooh! What a fumble!" Frannie jumped to her feet and clapped when the opposition dropped the ball and a Lincoln man ran with it, giving Lincoln several yards.

The crowd roared its appreciation. "Lincoln's ball on their 37. Third and 8," Page reported.

Frannie was busy trying to figure out what he meant when he nudged her. "Look at the strong right formation they're using."

"Look at how they're piling on," she exclaimed a few minutes later as one of the defense players was tackled. Page smiled. It was obvious to Frannie that unless she said something in footballese, Page hardly gave her a glance!

As the game neared half-time, her date once more became aware of her. "Hey, are you hungry? We'd better beat the crowd to the snack bar and get some hot dogs or something."

Pleased to be able to change the subject, she complied and followed him down the packed bleachers.

A small crowd was already swarming toward the snack bar. While clinging to Page's fingers, Frannie nearly collided with Gary Houseman.

"Frannie, hi." He grinned. "Great game, huh?"

Stunned, she muttered, "Oh, yeah. Great game."

Her fingers slid out of Page's. She saw his blond head ahead of her, but she was carried away from him by a tide of people.

Many people from Frannie's classes, boys and girls who had always acted as if she never existed, now noticed her with surprise.

Val and Bert crossed Frannie's path on their way back from the snack bar. "Hey, Fran, Page is looking for you. How'd you get lost?" Val talked loudly so that everyone could hear her.

"Look at this mob!" cried Frannie, who was not accustomed to large crowds.

"He said he'd go ahead and order you some food." She smiled and winked knowingly, which reminded Frannie that she would be expected to outline every detail of this night with her friends tomorrow.

Just then, she spotted Page moving toward her, arms above his head, balancing Cokes and hot dogs. "What a madhouse!"

"I'm surprised you're still in one piece," Frannie said, relieving him of half his burden. "Thanks for going to the trouble."

"Can't watch football on an empty stomach."

As they took their seats for the second half, Frannie realized she had just about exhausted her football repertoire. And no matter what subject was discussed, Page always managed to pull the conversation back to football.

"Well, you know," Frannie interjected when she got the opportunity, "that old saying— 'possession is nine-tenths of the law'?"

"Oh, yeah, I've heard it."

"With football, it's one hundred percent."

Page threw back his head and laughed. "You sure did your homework, Frannie!"

He would probably never guess how accurate he was about that.

Frannie was quiet through the remainder of the game as she concentrated on what the players were doing, tying together their actions with the descriptions she'd studied in the football books. She followed No. 18, Jason Billings, since he was the quarterback, and the only position she could recognize so far. Obviously, she would have to study far more, perhaps even go to more games.

Fortunately, Lincoln won. As they strolled out to Page's steel-blue Camaro, he turned to Frannie. "How about a Coke? We can talk about the game."

The suggestion made Frannie giggle, but since there was still an hour left until her curfew, she agreed.

Page chose a place called Tony's, a pizzeria near the high school. He ordered cokes and slices for both of them.

Tony's was a bright, cheerful place equipped with a blaring jukebox and small, oil-cloth covered tables. Bunches of plastic fruit hung from the ceiling next to unmatching light fixtures from different eras. To Frannie's eyes, it was a decorator's nightmare, but it was quite cozy nevertheless.

"You know, I used to play junior varsity. Fullback," Page told her with pride. She had wondered why he didn't play himself since he was so interested in the sport, but hadn't thought to ask him. "I messed up my knee last season—tore some ligaments. The doctor said I'd have to quit for awhile."

"Sorry to hear that." She now vaguely remembered seeing him on crutches last year.

He averted his eyes from hers and thoughtfully stirred the ice in his Coke. "Yeah, well those things happen. I'm lucky I wasn't hurt worse."

He talked more about the game until Frannie reminded him of her curfew.

Once outside, Page slung his arm casually around Frannie's shoulders. She could feel the warmth of his hand reach through the thin weave of her sweater, and was amazed at how pleasant his touch was to her. She didn't resist when, once they were parked outside her home, he gently kissed her goodnight.

"I had a real nice time tonight," he told her.

"Me, too."

"Maybe we can go out again sometime, okay?" He pushed a silk-blond strand of hair out of his eyes.

"Okay, sure."

He walked her to the front door and waited until she was safely inside.

"Well, how'd it go?" her dad asked the moment she stepped over the threshold. "And who won the game?"

"We won the game. And it went just fine, Dad," replied Frannie. Page's car sputtered to life outside.

"Was the boy nice?" her mother wanted to know.

"Yes, he was nice. But all he talked about was football."

Her parents laughed. Frannie flopped down on the sofa, glad and relieved at the same time—glad the night had been a success, and relieved that it was over at last.

Chapter Eleven

The phone rang six times Saturday morning before anyone answered it. Frannie finally rolled over, and through one eye glimpsed the time—seven o'clock. Who would call at seven on Saturday morning?

She groaned, realizing who it must be and dragged herself out of bed.

"Frannie, it's me, Charlene. How'd it go last night?"

"Couldn't you wait to find out?" Frannie rubbed her eyes, feeling groggy. It had taken her a long time to fall asleep after coming home. "It was fun, Charlene. I think I did okay."

"Terrific!" Charlene bubbled. "You know, people really noticed you."

"They did?"

"And after tonight, they won't ever forget you," breathed Charlene. "Did you finish the dress?"

"Almost. My mother and I have to put up the hem."

Frannie did a quick calculation of all the things she had to do—finish the dress, fix her hair, do her nails, go to the mall for some last minute items. There just wasn't time for another thing!

"I don't think I can handle the lesson today, Charlene. There's too much to do. I'll just have to practice at the dance, if anyone asks me." The thought of dancing in public awakened butterflies in her stomach.

"Not 'if,' Frannie, 'when,' " corrected her friend. "Val and I are meeting the guys at the dance, so we'll come by for you about seven."

Frannie could see that all hope of going back to sleep was lost as she hung up the phone. Instead, she curled up on her bed with her diary.

"I'm going to the Halloween dance tonight, and my dress is perfect. I'm so nervous because I hate dances. At least I know how to dance a little bit now.

"Last night Page suggested we go out again sometime, so I guess I did okay. All he talked about was football. He must need someone to listen to him. Charlene said people noticed me at the game. She thinks that's important. I'll let you know what happens at the dance, of course."

She closed the diary and went to the closet to examine her dress. It had a scooped neckline, a thin waist, and long, lace-trimmed sleeves. The skirt was very full, but not nearly as full as the original ones worn in the eighteenth century. Frannie's mother told her she'd have to wear a multitude of petticoats, plus an iron webbing to really be authentic. Women of those times had to walk sideways through doors, and when they sat down, they occupied enough space for three people. Frannie agreed that the original style would be highly impractical for the dance.

As it was, she would wear several petticoats. She was in love with the billowing, satiny folds of blue, and the way the lacey bodice pinched in at the waist. It wasn't an exact replica of the dress in Ronnie's poster, either. The poster girl's gown was high-necked and white, while Frannie's was, in her opinion, much more striking and appealing.

After breakfast, she and her mother spent the morning and part of the afternoon sewing. "Next time you decide to make a dress, Fran, leave some more time to make it, okay?"

Frannie realized her mother was largely responsible for the gown's completion. "Mom, I really appreciate your help," she said, setting down her needle so she could give her mother a big hug. "I never could've done this without you."

Joan Bronson smiled knowingly.

From the moment Frannie slipped the dress over her head, she felt transformed. Every button, every curve of lace was stitched down and in place, every fold of the blue skirt was perfect. Charlene and Val were over early with a curling iron to put the final touches on her ringlets and to inspect her makeup.

Charlene wore a bathing cap with antennae protruding from it for her bumblebee's head. It was already pinching off the circulation around her ears and forehead. Val was dressed as a "flapper" from the 1920's, wearing a sequined shift with bangles and beads draped from each arm and around her neck, topped off by a long scarf tied around her neck.

"Now I want a picture of all three of you lovelies," Mr. Bronson insisted, positioning his camera so that even Charlene's antennae fit into the snapshot.

They left Frannie's house around seven fifteen.

Charlene had a time of it getting her antennae into Valerie's car, causing Frannie and Val to laugh hysterically. By the time they reached the dance, Charlene announced she'd never dress up as a bumblebee again.

As they had planned, the girls chose the moment just before the band was announced to make their entrance.

The lights were dimming, and beneath the glittering, multi-mirrored ball in the center of the ceiling, couples and groups of teens were gathering. There was the excited murmur of conversation, and then, just as her friends had predicted, all eyes focused on Frannie, and a hush fell over the room.

Frannie could feel all of their eyes on her. Goosebumps traveled up both her arms, in spite of the shawl she wore draped around them.

Charlene nudged her. "Smile, Fran. Don't look so shocked."

She willed her face to smile, and at that moment the diamonds of lights splashed upon the walls by the twirling ball passed across her face, turning it radiant.

Lucy Marshall, dressed like a punk rocker, broke free of the crowd and came up to her. "Frances, I like your dress. Where did you get it?"

"I—I made it," stammered Frannie.

Before Lucy's obvious envy could touch Frannie, Gary Houseman, dressed as The Fonz, walked over and lifted her chilled hand. "Ehhhh, want to dance?" he inquired, with an absorbed smile.

The band struck its introductory chords, filling the room with sound. Frannie felt as if she were transformed into Cinderella as she lifted the folds of her skirt and followed Gary onto the dance floor.

Gary dropped Frannie's hand only after the band burst forth with its rocking beat, but he never took his eyes off her. She kept smiling, trying to think of other expressions that might work well when someone kept staring at you.

"You look so different," he shouted above the din.

She giggled, grateful for the distraction. "So do you."

He struck a Fonzie-like pose, and she laughed. Once again he took her hand and drew in close, even though the music was still fast. "You look like you stepped out of a history book," he told her. "Where did you get the outfit?"

"I made it," she replied, feeling a warm glow of satisfaction as his face lit up.

"You're kidding?" He held her at arms' length to get a better view of the dress.

"No, I'm not. My mother did help with it, too."

He nodded, as if he thought she must have had lots of help. It caused her to blush.

They danced two more numbers together before Page Garvey cut in.

"You look too pretty to take to a football game," he quipped, looking her over.

Frannie couldn't think of an answer, so she just smiled. Never in her life had she received so much attention from anyone! She and Page danced a slow dance, and she was immediately grateful for the dancing lessons. Closing her eyes, she glided across the floor without awkwardness, letting the slightest pressure of Page's hand on her waist guide her this way and that. It was fun, she had to admit.

When it was over, Frannie excused herself to get some punch. Halfway to the refreshment table, Val and Charlene cornered her.

"Frannie, Gary can't take his eyes off you," Val whispered, readjusting her scarf.

"Really?"

"The girls are just green over your dress. You couldn't have chosen a better costume!" Charlene beamed. "And the boys are going crazy, too. This is going to be the night of your life!"

"That's if Houseman lets her dance with anyone else!" Val giggled.

They made their way over to the punch table, where Frannie downed two glasses of the watery juice, before a boy masquerading as one of the Three Musketeers asked her to dance.

It struck Frannie just how silly it was to be dancing to a disco tune, each of them dressed in different period costumes. Her dancing partner was Cal Dudley, a handsome football player who was adorned with a fake mustache that had become undone and now bent at an odd angle. The feather plume in his hat jogged up and down wildly as he danced, and Frannie couldn't help but laugh.

"Do I look funny?" he asked her, pulling self-consciously at the ends of his mustache, in the effort to straighten it out.

"Oh, no, not at all," she fibbed, forcing herself to put on a straight face. She watched him smooth his light brown kinky hair back, being careful not to upset his Musketeer hat. From the sidelines, Charlene and Jason made a sign of approval. Cal must be someone they approved of.

Before the song was over, Adam Stone, dashingly disguised as Superman, cut in with, "May I rescue you?"

"Sure!" Frannie blurted out. Truly, he was about the best-looking Superman she'd ever seen. With a dramatic flourish, he spun her into his arms.

"Where've you been all my life, Frannie?" Adam grinned down at her, white teeth flashing.

Frannie shrugged. How were you supposed to answer that kind of question?

Looking over his shoulder, she became aware of other people looking at them. They must be looking at Adam, she decided—with his bright red cape and close-fitting Superman suit, he was sinfully handsome.

As Adam whirled Frannie around and around, she caught a fleeting glimpse of Lucy Marshall's angry scowl—an expression that didn't go well with the shimmering pink, skin-tight pants and leopard-print leotard she wore.

When the number was over, Superman bowed gallantly and thanked Frannie for the dance. She quickly retreated to the sideline, which she hadn't seen much of all evening. What a change!

Soon her friends joined her. "Adam's trying to smooth everything over with Lucy," Patti, dressed as Catwoman, reported. "Boy, is she ever mad at you!"

Frannie was shocked. "What did *I* do?"

"All you did was look irresistible!"

Patti's boyfriend Scott arrived on the scene just

then, outfitted as Batman, to capture Catwoman for the next dance. "Frannie, you look great," he exclaimed, shaking his head in wonderment.

"See," affirmed Charlene. "What did we tell you?"

Next Fred Brown asked Frannie to dance. He hadn't worn a costume himself, but he, too, thought Frannie's was incredible. He danced the next two dances with her.

The band broke for intermission, and Frannie searched the room, checking out the costumes. There was a Wonder Woman, an anonymous Snoopy, several football players who had simply worn their football gear as costumes, a karate expert, a few witches and of course, one or two ghosts. She noticed, with a twinge of disappointment, that Ronnie Schell wasn't there.

"May I sit with you?" Gary Houseman asked her.

Frannie was sitting on a folding chair, giving her feet a rest. "Oh, sure, go ahead," she said enthusiastically, gathering up the voluminous folds of her skirt which draped over the adjoining seats.

Gary took a comb out of the pocket of his black leather jacket and began to comb his slicked-back hair. "You know, I think your costume is the best. I bet you win first prize." The gold flecks in his eyes were more pronounced once the lights dimmed.

"For what?" she wanted to know.

"For the best costume, naturally."

"Really? I mean, no one told me they gave out prizes."

"Yeah. They do it every year. I forget all the

categories, Best, Worst, Most Original, stuff like that."

She briefly wondered why Patti, Val and Charlene had never mentioned it. Did they think it would frighten her off, perhaps?

Mr. Carniglia, Frannie's art teacher and one of the dance chaperones, climbed onto the stage and read off the categories. "We're ready to announce the winners for the Best Costume, the Worst, the Funniest Costume, the Most Original and the Most Beautiful."

Gary reached over and covered her hand with his. "You're going to win something."

"Oh, no, not me," protested Frannie quickly.

Mr. Carniglia slit the envelope with one of his long fingernails. "For Best Costume," he read, "it's Adam Stone!"

There was a loud, feminine cheering section led by Lucy Marshall as Adam swaggered to the stage to receive his award.

"Who judges this contest anyway?" Frannie wanted to know.

"Teachers—all the chaperones," said Gary.

"The Worst Costume award goes to Wendy Cabral." Wendy played her part to the hilt: wearing striped pajamas and foam curlers in her hair, she yawned and stretched her way onto the stage.

"Charlene McDaniels gets the award for the Funniest Costume!" Mr. Carniglia called out. Frannie cheered loudly for her friend, who, without a doubt, deserved that award.

"For Most Original, we have a couple," Mr. Carniglia announced. "Patti Davis and Scott

Winchell." Everyone laughed as Catwoman and Batman hugged each other on stage.

"Last, but not least—" said Mr. Carniglia, prefacing his next announcement. "The Most Beautiful Costume award goes to Frances Bronson!"

Frannie's jaw dropped. She was numbly aware of Gary nudging her gently. "Get up, Frannie. Get your award!"

"Congratulations, Frannie!" people called out to her, as she walked up to the stage to accept her award.

Carefully, she lifted her skirt to scale the three narrow steps to the stage. Mr. Carniglia presented her with the tiny trophy and shook her limp hand. "Congratulations, Frannie."

"Thank you," she whispered.

The room buzzed with excitement. At the bottom of the steps, Gary stood and offered her his hand. Frannie couldn't believe this was happening to her. She felt as if she'd been transported into someone else's magical body, wearing someone else's magical dress, to take part in a dream.

"Congratulations, Frannie," Gary told her. With a crooked smile still upon his lips, he bent to kiss her cheek.

The dry, freshly shaven roughness of his cheek thrilled her. "I'm so surprised," she admitted. Gary took her hand and led her onto the dance floor.

"Why? You're the best-looking girl here tonight," he said.

Her face grew hot. Frannie had still not learned

how to accept compliments gracefully, so she didn't respond. She closed her eyes instead, and let the rhythm of the music move her, enjoying Gary's closeness and the sweeping sensation of the two of them gliding beneath the twirling, starry ball that illuminated the dance floor.

Chapter Twelve

"I've told you all about the dance, Diary, but now I'm wondering if it all really happened. Maybe if I pinch myself hard I'll discover I was just dreaming the whole thing."

Frannie sighed heavily, her pen between her teeth. When she closed her eyes, she saw herself at the dance, the lights picking up the satiny sheen of her dress, and the appreciative look in her partners' eyes.

Was it all a dream? she wondered. Could people really see her as a completely new person, just because she had on a different dress?

Charlene said that everyone was talking about her, about how cute she is, how nice and how come we didn't notice her before. Just being at the dance was great for her reputation, her friend insisted. A girl has to be seen around, she has to mingle with the crowd. How else will anyone know who she is?

"Winning the contest helped too, Fran," Charlene assured her. "That dress was the best. And making it yourself was a stroke of genius."

Early Sunday morning Charlene came over clutching a long wall calendar to her chest.

"What's that for?"

"It's to keep track of your dates," explained Charlene. "You're going to be really busy from now on."

"Isn't this going a little far, Charlene?" Frannie helped Charlene out of her coat. "I mean, what makes you so sure?"

"You didn't believe me when I said the plan would work, so why should you believe me now when I tell you you're going to be very busy from now on?" She grinned mysteriously. "Anyway, I know something you don't know."

"What?"

"I don't know if I should tell you this," Charlene teased. "Maybe I should let it be a surprise."

"Tell me! I can't stand the suspense!"

"Jason told me Cal Dudley's going to ask you out." Frannie stared at her in disbelief. "You know," Charlene said. "Mr. Musketeer."

Frannie had known immediately who he was. Handsome, popular Calvin Dudley wanted to ask her out? Her, plain old Frannie Bronson? "You're kidding. Why me?"

"Frannie, he's crazy about you, that's why. And he couldn't believe you're not going with anyone."

Frannie nearly spilled her cup of hot chocolate. This was too incredible to be true. But she was wide awake—this was no dream.

"You need some more dancing lessons, and I think you should keep studying football," Charlene went on. "But you don't really need a daily schedule to follow anymore. I think you can handle yourself just fine."

"I'm glad you have so much confidence in me," Frannie shivered, not feeling very confident at all. She felt relieved that the daily "talking to boys" schedule was over, though. She was beginning to worry that the boys would become suspicious of her if it continued too much longer.

Frannie stayed in her room most of the day doing homework, just like old times, she thought. Just like old times, except that Cal Dudley would soon be asking her out. That would be the second date of her entire life.

She was so nervous she could barely concentrate. It was one thing to go to a football game where you didn't have to talk too much, but quite another to go on a date somewhere else. Where would they go? What would she say? She didn't belong to any clubs or groups, so what could she talk about? What a wonderful football player he was? But she didn't even know what position he played. Anyway, that was only about three minutes' worth of conversation.

Frannie found herself hoping he'd change his mind and not ask her. It would be easier all the way around.

Just before dinner, the phone rang. Frannie's heart skipped a beat—she'd been waiting on tenterhooks all day and could stand the wait no longer. "Frannie, it's for you!"

"Hi, do you know who this is?" It was a boy, but Frannie couldn't place his voice, although she assumed it was Cal.

"No."

"It's Gary, Gary Houseman, you know? Fonzie at the dance."

Stunned, Frannie gripped the receiver tightly. "Oh, uh, sure. Hi, Gary."

"Well, Frannie, I was wondering if you could go to a party next week, on Halloween night?"

Frannie was remembering how his arms felt around her as they danced and how attentive he was. "I'd like to," she replied.

"Good. I'll pick you up around seven-thirty, okay?"

"Okay." Frannie hung up the receiver in a state of shocked bliss. A date—another date. With Gary of all people! She briefly remembered Charlene's wall calendar and couldn't help smiling to herself. It looked like she would need it after all.

"Who was that?" her mother inquired.

"A boy from school. He asked me to go to a party Halloween night," Frannie replied, trying to keep her smile from growing too wide.

"That's wonderful, Fran!" Joan Bronson exclaimed, giving Frannie's shoulders an affectionate squeeze. "Was it someone from the dance last night?"

"Yes."

"Did I hear our Frannie's going out on another date?" her father bellowed from the hallway. He entered the kitchen beaming. "I told you you'd be a hit in that dress! With a trophy to prove it!"

"Oh, Dad," Frannie sighed, knowing that everyone in his office would hear about her on Monday morning. Before she could escape, she sat through another five agonizing minutes of questioning: What's his name? What classes do you have together? Is he a "nice" boy?

Finally, with the rhythm of one of last night's songs tripping through her brain, she pirouetted into her bedroom.

Charlene's wall calendar still lay on her bed. Frannie located a tin of tacks in her desk drawer and hung the calendar on the inside of her closet door. Then she wrote in her first entry under Saturday: *Gary, 7:30 pm.*

All of a sudden she remembered that Cal Dudley hadn't even called her yet!

Chapter Thirteen

"Congratulations on your award, Frannie," Fred Brown told her first thing Monday morning when they met at their lockers.

Frannie's pleasure shone on her face. "Thanks, Freddie," she beamed. "It sure was a surprise to me."

He cocked his head to one side and looked somewhat puzzled. "It was? You were the cutest girl there."

She blushed and quickly turned to get some books out of her locker.

As she hurried down the hall to her first class, Frannie was amazed at how many people noticed her. "Oh, hi, Frannie!" called Marilyn Blake, one of the cheerleaders, as if Frannie were some long lost friend. They'd never exchanged two words before.

She saw Ronnie Schell unpinning one of his posters from the wall.

"Congratulations, Frannie!" Page Garvey hollered and winked at her.

Ronnie turned around and glanced at Frannie as she passed. "Hi," she ventured, her heart pounding in her ears.

He nodded, and with a small, shy smile said, "Hi."

Frannie sailed into algebra, unmindful of Gary Houseman's eyes following her. She was a new Frannie, someone who was noticeable around school. She had been unafraid to say "hi" to Ronnie this morning, and that was really something for her! Her throat hadn't clogged up as it had in the past, and the word just flowed right out, as she'd always dreamed it might someday! This must be the self-confidence Charlene talked about, she realized. And Charlene had been right—she *had* missed so much because of her shyness.

Cal Dudley approached Frannie as she came out of the snack bar line at lunch and asked her to go to a movie with him. "I'm busy Saturday," she was proud to tell him. "Maybe Friday." How casual she was!

Cal hesitated. "Uh, Friday's my game. How about Sunday?"

Frannie wondered how her parents would react to her going out on a Sunday night. So far they hadn't mentioned dating rules, since she'd never dated before. "Sure," she accepted, although she wasn't really sure.

"I think the whole school knows about the new star of the junior class," Val reported over lunch.

"Everybody's congratulated me," Frannie said, "even girls I've never talked to before."

"Lucy Marshall's just green and she hates you," Charlene said, grinning wickedly.

"Oh, no! I don't want anyone to hate me."

"Don't worry, Fran. It's good for her, and I think it'll be good for you, too. As long as you don't try and crowd in on Adam Stone, that is," Charlene explained. "You might as well get used to it. Now that you've been 'discovered,' other girls are going to get jealous."

"That's just the way it is," Val shrugged. "When all the boys start going after you, the girls start wishing you had a big wart on your nose or something."

Frannie still couldn't imagine herself as someone girls would be envious of. She was an ordinary girl, certainly no prettier than the most popular girls at Lincoln High, so why would they be jealous?

At the beginning of fifth period, Adam Stone struck a dramatic pose in the doorway, and announced: "Frannie Bronson, the ce-le-bri-ty!" as Frannie walked into the room.

If looks could kill, she thought, the one Lucy Marshall shot her way would've burned a hole through her. She shuddered, wishing she could tell Adam to keep quiet. As nice as it was to get attention, she didn't want Lucy—or anyone for that matter—to hate her.

When she took her seat, Frannie stole a sidelong glance at Ronnie. The expression he wore as he looked at Adam was one of puzzlement.

Maybe now that everyone else notices me, she dreamed, he'll notice me, too.

Joan Bronson glared at Frannie's new wall calendar. "Why didn't you ask us if it was all right for you to make these plans?" she demanded.

"Mom, nobody's ever asked me out before. You think I'm going to turn these boys down?" squeaked Frannie, tears brimming in her eyes at the mere thought of having to erase her dates from the calendar.

"You've got a date Wednesday after school, Friday, Saturday, Sunday and one next Thursday. When do you plan on doing your homework?"

Frannie hadn't considered that. But somehow, she figured she'd have time to fit it in. "I'll manage."

"No, you won't," her mother said firmly. "You'll cancel Thursday and Sunday. And, your father and I have decided you'll have to limit your phone calls."

"But Mom! Nobody else's parents limit their calls!"

She smiled one of her maddening, all-knowing smiles. "I'm sure we're not the first parents to think of it. We have to have rules, Frannie. Five minutes per phone call, and no weeknight dating."

"I hope you know you're ruining my whole life! Nobody's going to ask me out now—just when I'm getting started!"

"We're not ruining your life, Frannie," Mrs. Bronson protested. "The boys won't run away."

"You're wrong. They will," she cried.

"No, Frannie. If they aren't willing to invite you out again, then they're not really worth going out with at all," her mother said quietly. "There are other things in life besides boys. I don't want you neglecting your schoolwork on their behalf."

"I can't believe I'm talking to the same mother! I hate you!" Frannie exploded, her fists clenched into knots.

Joan Bronson's face clouded, and she closed the door of her daughter's room softly behind her, leaving Frannie alone with her anger.

Frannie stared at her calendar. What an impressive social life she had lined up, until her mother had to go and wreck everything. Wednesday after school she was going to get a snack with Fred. Friday was the football game with Page. Saturday was Halloween with Gary, and on Sunday Frannie was supposed to go out with Cal Dudley. Gary had also invited her to a school play the following Thursday, and now she would have to cancel.

Carefully, she erased Sunday and Thursday's plans from the calendar. She refused to eat dinner, yet she set the table for her parents, in complete silence. When Charlene phoned, Frannie made sure her parents heard every sharp word. "I can only talk for five minutes, Charlene. And I also have to limit my dating, besides my phone calls."

"Oh, yeah?"

Frannie told her about cancelling the two dates.

"Well, just be sure to let Cal know you're still interested. He's in demand. Tell him you'll go out with him next weekend," suggested her friend.

Frannie wondered why he was in such demand, for he didn't really appeal to her, but it was nice to have such a popular boy interested in her. When she hung up, she turned to catch her parents studying her with that someday-you're-going-to-thank-us look. Disgusted, she shuffled into her bedroom, slammed the door and put on a Stones record in the hopes that the sound would separate her from them more completely.

As she set her hair later, she thought over the events of the past few days. After she'd gotten home from school earlier that afternoon, she'd talked to Page on the phone for about a half hour. Or more correctly, he'd talked to her. Then her mother had come home from work and had asked her to get off the phone. Last night, Gary had tied up the line for nearly an hour before Frannie's father had told her to get off. Charlene, Val and Patti all had teased her about being unreachable.

After setting out her clothes for the next day, Frannie opened her diary. *"I'm so angry I could scream. Now that I know how to accept dates, how do I turn them down? I'm a different person and my parents don't know me. They still think of me as the dependent baby I was before."*

She let the angry words spew out onto the paper. *"I feel like I'm walking a tightrope between being a nobody and a somebody, and any minute something will happen to make me a nobody again."*

Frannie read over what she'd written. She was different, yes, but not in all ways. She was still not very secure about herself, still very shy deep down inside. In that one way, she was still the same old Frannie.

Chapter Fourteen

Wednesday's after school date with Fred Brown went pretty well, as far as Frannie was concerned. Fred was an easy person to talk to —or listen to. He talked about his favorite science fiction books, the project he was building for the science fair and his favorite teachers. Frannie, in all honesty, didn't have too much to offer to the conversation, so she was glad she was a good listener. They both ordered chocolate shakes, and Fred seemed content to talk while Frannie sipped.

Frannie's football game date with Page was almost a carbon copy of the first one, except that now she knew a little more about football. Watching the game taught her much more than reading about it, and she even suspected she might begin to like it.

On Halloween night, Gary arrived at Frannie's house dressed in his Fonzie costume.

"This isn't how I usually dress, Mr. and Mrs. Bronson," he quickly assured Frannie's parents.

"You do look like an odd couple though," Mr. Bronson teased. "Where're the two of you off to?"

"A party at one of my friends' house," replied Gary. Once they were in the car and he'd introduced Frannie to Julie Bernstein and Ray Stills, who were doubling with them, he said, "You might not know anyone at the party, Frannie."

Frannie stiffened underneath her special dress. As Gary eased the car away from the curb, she wanted to tell him to stop. "Where is it? It's not given by someone from school?" she managed in a quavery voice. She heard Julie giggle in the back seat.

Gary grinned and draped an arm around her shoulders. "My friend Kim's parents are gone for the weekend, so we're gonna help him celebrate. It'll be a great party."

She felt a sudden, unfamiliar twist of fear in her stomach at the thought of entering a crowd of strangers. But if she didn't go through with this date, another part of her reasoned, what would become of her brand-new self and her new, hard-won reputation?

Julie, Ray and Gary joked and laughed together during the ride to Kim's place. Frannie made a few efforts to join in, but everything she said seemed unnatural and forced, and she just couldn't relax.

The party was in full swing when they arrived. Kim's parents' home was a large ranch-style house equipped with a pool table and complete bar, which everyone helped themselves to. Frannie couldn't help wondering what Kim's parents would have done if they knew about this party. A dining table and chairs had been pushed to one side to make room for dancing, which Gary led her to right away, sensing her discomfort.

This was nothing like the Halloween dance at

all, Frannie thought in dismay. The stereo was turned up to ear-splitting volume. Nearly everyone was dressed in jeans or unimaginative costumes, which only increased Frannie's feeling of being out of place, outfitted as she was in her Revolutionary War gown. She noticed people growing sillier and drunker as the night wore on, and she worried that maybe she was keeping Gary from having a good time with his friends.

"Are you having a good time?" he asked her all too often.

She forced a bright smile. "Oh, yes, thank you," she kept repeating.

When they were ready to leave, Gary and Frannie wove their way through the unfamiliar rooms looking for Julie and Ray. "It's too early to go," Julie cried out drunkenly when they found the couple in the den. Ray shrugged in helpless agreement, so Frannie and Gary left them at the party.

"I'd still like to take you to the play next week," Gary told her when they were in the car alone. "To kind of make up for this. It wasn't such a hot party."

"It was okay, honest," she insisted, then realized how hollow that sounded. She really felt that the party was loud, raucous and ugly in comparison to the softly lit dream dance at school, where she fit in perfectly. Here she stood out like a sore thumb, like a girl who had stepped out of a time machine, from the looks people gave her. She and Gary had danced like robots all evening, very uncomfortable with each other. Though she had closed her eyes and tried to recapture that wonderful mood, it just wouldn't take much to make her cry. "I can't go out on weeknights, remember?" she reminded him, and he nodded quietly.

At Frannie's house, Gary turned off the ignition and pulled her gently toward him. His lips found hers quickly and he kissed her tenderly. Frannie's hand stole around to the back of his neck where his hair curled over his collar. She touched it, just once, like she'd wanted to so many times in class. Still holding her, Gary kissed her forehead, and the warm glow of romance flickered in her once more. Maybe everything's all right, after all, she thought.

Toting sketchpads, stools, charcoal and sharpened pencils, the fifth period art class marched along Beech Street in search of the perfect Victorian style house to sketch. So many of the old structures were dilapidated, with large areas of gingerbreading missing and broken cornices jutting over peeling paint, but Mr. Carniglia didn't mind that. What he looked for, and what he taught the class to look for, were houses with "character," not candidates for *House Beautiful*.

Frannie walked close to Mr. Carniglia, not so much because she wanted to hear what he had to say, but because she wanted to escape from Adam Stone. Charlene had heard via the grapevine that Adam had his eye on her, and although Lucy Marshall had no claim on Adam, the last thing Frannie needed was to become involved with a boy someone else liked.

Sticking close to Mr. Carniglia also had another positive benefit—it put Frannie much closer to Ronnie. She stood directly behind him, memorizing each seam in the back of his brown and beige ski jacket as if it were the most important thing in the world.

"What do you think of this house, Ron?" Mr. Carniglia stopped in front of a tall, rambling structure with a postage stamp front yard hemmed in by a wrought-iron fence.

Ronnie shrugged modestly. How could he be so casual about a teacher asking for his opinion! Frannie wondered. "It's good, I think," replied Ronnie. "I wouldn't mind doing some Christmas cards of it."

"Pen and ink Christmas cards?" Frannie cut in excitedly. "I think those are marvelous." She stopped suddenly, surprised at the sound of her own voice.

Ronnie turned around. Under his soft gray gaze, Frannie wanted to melt. "Yeah, that's what I had in mind. Maybe with a touch of color—a tree in the window or something like that." He gestured with one hand to the old shuttered windows.

Frannie took a secret pleasure in the knowledge that she had already thought to do pen and ink cards this year. Ever since she was able to pick up a pencil, she had drawn her own cards, but she didn't want to boast about it to Ronnie. It seemed too calculated to her.

Frannie set down her stool next to Ronnie's while other students filtered off down the street looking for other houses. As Adam passed, she felt a tension dissolve, and she could fully enjoy Ronnie's presence next to her.

With relative ease, his hand recorded what his eye saw. Frannie was entranced with the old house coming to life on his pad, so much so that she nearly forgot to do her own sketch. "I love the posters you did for the Halloween dance," she told him. "Especially the one of the Revolutionary War couple."

"Thanks," Ronnie said, eyes fixed on the house.

"In fact," Frannie chattered on nervously, "that poster inspired my Halloween costume, I liked it so much."

"Really?" She thought she detected the faintest smile upon his lips, but it vanished almost instantly, leaving her to wonder if she'd seen it at all.

She wished they could sit together forever, for what she felt for Ronnie was a magnetism stronger than anything she felt for other boys she knew. Maybe it was because they held similar interests, but whatever it was, each fact Frannie learned about Ronnie made her feelings run deeper.

When it was time to head back to class, Ronnie grabbed his stool and hurried ahead of her. Frannie felt desolate, as if the sun had suddenly ducked behind a dark cloud. A part of her wanted to jump up and run after him, yelling, "Hey, wait for me!" As self-confident as she had become, however, she was not ready to do that yet. So she dawdled, and, not surprisingly, Adam Stone fell into step beside her.

"I've been waiting for a chance to talk to you." He grinned as if she should be pleased he deemed her important enough to seek out. "Can we be friends?"

Instant irritation pricked Frannie. The flirtatious look he gave her indicated he was seeking more than her friendship and that he was confident she would jump at the chance!

As cooly as she could manage, she answered, "We already are friends, Adam."

The confidence slid from his face momentarily, but he quickly recovered with a wide smile. "Frannie, a guy could fall in love with you," he said over his shoulder as he walked off.

Frannie saw a different expression dawn on Freddie's face the very next day when she had to tell him her Saturday night was already booked up. "I'm free Friday, though," she said, hoping he would ask her out and rescue her from another football game with Page.

Fred, however, was not as confident nor as cocky as Adam. His face changed as an evolution of thought took place, which left a gaping, empty hole in the conversation. "Friday's just fine," was his slow answer, but she sensed he wasn't completely happy with the arrangement. "Can I ask you who you're going out with Saturday?"

"Cal Dudley," she said. "We were supposed to go out last week, but—"

"But you couldn't fit him in," Fred supplied darkly.

Frannie smoothed her damp palms down the front of her gray wool skirt. She didn't know what to say.

"I guess you're one of those girls who doesn't like to get tied down, huh?"

Her face grew hot. Well, was she that type of girl?

"I've only just started dating, Fred," she said in her defense. "I—I don't really know how to answer that question, to be honest, because I don't know if I'd want to be tied down or not."

He took a bite of his hamburger and nodded, as though he understood, but his words had unsettled Frannie more than he could know.

When she arrived home, she made a beeline for her calendar to update it for the weekend and then recorded the day's events in her diary. *"Maybe,"* she paused, unsure whether to commit her suspicion to writing, *"Fred said that because he is getting serious about me, which I don't want. I mean I like him. He's a good friend, but I don't feel romantic about him. In fact . . ."* The diary had the ability to squeeze absolute truth out of Frannie, as if it possessed some magic power. She hesitated, in one way wanting to hold back her real feelings, but in another way, anxious to voice them somehow. *"I don't feel really truly romantic about any of the boys I've been dating. I felt that way at the dance, with the dress, the attention, and all that, but I didn't feel that way about any one person."*

But then Frannie thought of Ronnie and how he spoke, what it was like to stand near him. She imagined for a moment what it would be like to experience his arms around her. *"Diary—maybe there is one person I'd like to get serious about."*

She lifted her hand for a second and the pages of her diary flipped backward. She glanced down and the words, written only a few weeks before, jumped right up at her: *"Will I ever have a special boyfriend?"*

"That's what I really want—a special boyfriend," she scribbled. *"Someone like Patti's Scott*

is to her, like Jason is to Charlene—a real romance. Sure, they might break up some day, but what they have right now is wonderful.

"I love dating, but I want that wonderfulness. Ronnie is special, different from all the other boys. If only I could get his attention..."

Chapter Fifteen

"You have to bring a date to Marilyn Blake's party. It's couples only," Charlene informed Frannie. They sat side by side in the high school cafeteria, their party invitations spread out next to their lunches. "Who will you invite? I know Cal would love to go with you. He told Jason he's crazy about you."

Frannie grinned. She certainly was in demand. Was it her imagination, or had the boys become more interested in her since her parents had made the dating rules? Could her mother be right after all? Charlene said it was possible. Just last week she had been asked out by Page, Freddie, Gary and Cal. Each one was popular, and out of the four, she could accept only two. It was good for her ego, she had to admit. No more staying home on weekends. That chapter of her life was over forever, it seemed.

Friday night Frannie attended the Science Fair with Fred, who won an honorable mention for his entry. Saturday night she and Cal went to see a movie that they both enjoyed. Afterward he took her to a burger place for a Coke. They talked about the movie, and about how well he did at Friday's game, which of course she hadn't seen.

How crestfallen big, soft-eyed Cal had looked when she told him she hadn't seen him perform!

When they arrived at her house, Cal leaned over to kiss her, but she quickly slid across the seat with a hasty "thank you for a nice evening" and hurried up the walk. Frannie could only imagine the pouty look on his face after she left him.

The trouble was, she decided, he was probably accustomed to having his own way. Girls generally didn't turn him down, so it came as quite a shock when one did.

"If I were you, I'd go with Cal," Charlene urged, handing her a segment of orange, bringing her back to the present.

"Maybe I will," said Frannie, but she wasn't thinking of Cal. She was thinking this would be the perfect opportunity to ask Ronnie Schell.

Ronnie was on his hands and knees searching for something in the floor cabinet when Frannie breezed into the art room, looking for him. She wanted to ask him before her courage shriveled up, so she knelt down beside him and placed her books gently on the floor. "Ronnie?" she ventured, her voice an octave higher than usual.

Ronnie started, whacking his head on the inside of the cupboard. "What?" he demanded, when anyone else would've cursed.

"Oh, I'm sorry, but I was wondering," Frannie was babbling, powerless to stop. Expectation ran like a silver thread through her voice when she asked: "Would you like to go to Marilyn Blake's party with me? It's Saturday night."

Ronnie studied her solemnly while rubbing his sore head. He blushed as he answered, "Well, I can't, I'm busy that night." Then, as an after-thought, he added, "Thanks anyway." Quickly he rose, and made his way across the room to where Mr. Carniglia was wiping a clay-speckled counter.

Heartsick, Frannie stared at a wide crack in the linoleum. She felt as if the wind had just been knocked out of her. Why had he said no? Immediately she was jealous of whatever he planned to do that night.

But her feelings swung full circle as she began to really wonder why he had refused her, when so many popular boys were so anxious to go out with her. One look in the mirror vanquished any fears she might have had regarding her looks. She was, by most people's standards, an attractive, pretty girl. She had been spending a lot of time on her appearance, setting her hair, choosing her clothes carefully, doing her fingernails. She was smart, talented—all those things Charlene had tried to tell her about herself, she now realized were true.

So why, then, didn't Ronnie Schell see these things?

"You look good tonight," Cal complimented Frannie.

"Thanks," she replied. "So do you." She was glad she had chosen the soft pink boucle sweater and maroon skirt for Marilyn's party, instead of something more casual. And Cal looked nice, too, wearing a sweater and dark brown slacks instead of the usual letterman jacket he always wore with jeans.

Frannie guessed they must make an attractive couple as they stood on the flagstone porch of Marilyn Blake's home, to be ushered in quickly by Marilyn's mother.

"Go right down the hall. Everyone's in the family room," she directed.

The hallway opened onto a large, comfortable room, bordered by worn couches, a TV, a stereo, and a ping pong table, on which now sat a huge cut-glass bowl of punch. Frannie thought it was properly called a "family" room, noting the school pictures and awards decorating the knotty pine-wood walls.

"Oh, hi, Frannie and Cal!" Marilyn greeted them. "Glad you two could make it."

"Wouldn't miss it," Cal mumbled, grinning at her.

"Me, either," parroted Frannie.

"Make yourselves at home," Marilyn went on, her eyes locked with Cal's. Frannie was pleased that her date was so impressive. "There's punch over here, and lots of good albums . . ." Marilyn chattered on excitedly.

"Thanks a lot," Cal said, moving into the thick of the crowd.

The party consisted entirely of Lincoln High kids, the popular crowd Frannie was just beginning to know. She was relieved to see Lucy Marshall there with Adam Stone. Jo Curry, another girl who had dated Adam, pulled Frannie aside. "Tell me, what's he like?"

Frannie wasn't sure at first about whom she was talking. "Oh, you mean, Cal?" Jo nodded furiously. "Oh, he's very nice. We had a great time at a movie last weekend," she said noncommittally, realizing that whatever she told Jo wouldn't remain a secret.

Jo smiled and whispered confidentially. "You're really lucky to be going out with him. I hear he's really crazy about you."

Frannie giggled. "Really? He's never told me that!"

"Oh, but can't you tell?" Jo persisted. "Just the way he looks at you."

He did look at her a certain way, she thought.

Someone put on a slow record, and Jo and Frannie moved apart. Marilyn placed three lit candles on the table, while her boyfriend Don switched off the lights.

"You wanna dance, Frannie?" Cal was at her side. He crushed a styrofoam cup in one meaty hand while awaiting her answer.

"Sure." She watched him pitch the crumpled cup into a nearby waste can. "Do you play basketball, too?" Frannie asked as they began to dance.

"Yeah, but I'm not on the team or anything," Cal said seriously. "My thing is strictly football, you know."

"Well, you ought to be on the team, you shoot good baskets," she teased. Cal didn't see the joke. "Maybe you could get one of those executive baskets you place over waste cans."

"Oh, yeah." Cal managed a chuckle, but Frannie knew her joke went flat. She couldn't think of another topic of conversation, unless of course, it was football, so she squeezed her eyes shut and let Cal lead her around the dance floor. He was a smooth dancer, but he was so much taller than she that her neck ached by the time the music stopped.

The lights blinked on and some of the couples drifted over to the refreshments. A fast song ripped into the room and Cal took Frannie's hand, then spun her around to the staccato beat. In mid-spin, Frannie saw someone that sent her heart slamming into her throat. In the corner, next to the potato chips, was Ronnie Schell!

Ronnie held out a cup of punch to Arlene Paine, a studious girl who was neither popular nor even good-looking. They stood together in the corner, as if they were dates, talking about something that they obviously felt was far more interesting than what was going on at the party.

Then Frannie remembered—Marilyn's invitation stipulated that you couldn't come to her party alone. So Ronnie must have asked Arlene, instead of taking Frannie. Ronnie must have received the invitation—Marilyn would never have given one to Arlene.

As the music rose to a final crescendo, so did Frannie's puzzlement and anger. Why did Ronnie take her to the party instead? Even without her two-inch-thick glasses, shaggy pixie haircut, severe, square chin and twenty extra pounds, Arlene was nobody's ideal date, Frannie surmised cattily. There was just no way Ronnie could choose Arlene over Frannie. It didn't make sense at all!

Suddenly Marilyn's rose-pink punch and bakery-bought cookies formed a hard lump in Frannie's stomach. She felt sick—with jealousy. All she wanted to do was go home and cry.

But she couldn't. Cal whirled her into his arms, then spun her away, damp brown corkscrews of hair falling loose across his forehead. He was having a good time, and Frannie didn't want to spoil it for him. When the dance ended, he wrapped both arms around her in a big bear hug which was nearly suffocating. "That was great, Frannie!" he exclaimed. "Let's get something to drink, then dance some more."

Cal was more animated than Frannie had ever seen him, but she couldn't help wishing she was in Ronnie's arms, instead of Cal's.

Ronnie and Arlene got in line behind Cal and Frannie. Frannie wanted to say hi, but she couldn't bear to look into Ronnie's face, fearful that everything she was thinking about him would show. Without looking at Ronnie, she reached in front of him for the cocktail napkins. "Excuse me," she said formally.

"Sure," responded Ronnie dully. Was it as uncomfortable for him as it was for her? she wondered.

"Thanks, Frannie. You're a doll." Cal accepted the napkins, talking louder than he needed to. "I've got to be careful I don't slop this down the front of my good shirt." What a gross thing to say, thought Frannie.

"Your mother might kill you," one of the girls teased him, and he laughed.

Val bustled over to say hi. "Haven't had a chance to talk to you, Miss Twinkletoes." She winked. Bert slid his arm around her waist, and Frannie sensed he wanted Val all to himself.

"There's always tomorrow, Val," she said. Bert

smiled and led his girl out to the middle of the floor.

"C'mon, Frannie, I wanna dance with you," Cal said, pulling her close. The lights went out, leaving only the soft, flickering candlelight and a sweet melody that wove a mood of romance into the party. Frannie hoped the mood didn't touch Arlene and Ronnie.

"This is beautiful, I love that song," Cal whispered, lowering his head so that he could get close to Frannie's ear. "You know, I remember one time when I was making this lateral pass . . ."

Frannie clamped her mouth shut over a giggle. Here goes the romance, ended on the twenty-five yard line she joked to herself. Sure, she liked Cal—he was good company—but love and romance to him were second or maybe even third to football and the adulation he received from his performance on the field. The girls who were crazy about him were probably adoring him in the same way one would love Shaun Cassidy of Mark Hamill—not how you would love a real, live-in-the-flesh boyfriend. And not the way Bert loved Val, for instance. That was special, sweet—the kind of love she hungered for.

Chapter Sixteen

"What's so great about Ronnie Schell? I don't even know who he is!" Charlene exclaimed, eyeing Frannie with pure horror.

"Sure you do. He was at Marilyn's party . . . with Arlene," Frannie said, wincing at the thought of the two of them together.

"Oh, him," Charlene said disdainfully. "I don't get it, Fran."

"He paints those fantastic posters you see around school," Frannie explained. "He's really talented . . . and sensitive."

"But he's not popular, and there's got to be a reason. I don't understand you, Fran. Cal's mad for you, and half the best guys in school want to take you out. But is that good enough for you? Oh, noooo. You go off and pine over somebody with a paintbrush!" Charlene's dark eyes flashed dangerously bright.

"I just said I'd like to go out with him, that's all. I like him. Is there something wrong with that?"

All of a sudden, Frannie wished she hadn't confided in Charlene. Sure, they were best friends, but this was evidently a sore subject with Charlene, who had very definite opinions about who was good to go out with. Also, she didn't want to sound as if she were complaining about her dates.

"It's not that I don't like Cal and the others. I do, honest. It's just that I don't have a lot in common with them. Don't you understand?"

"No, I don't. How can you put down the most popular guys in our class? Don't you realize what you've got now?"

"Maybe if you knew Ronnie a little better, you'd see what I mean."

"Maybe," returned Charlene. "But if he's the kind of guy who'd choose Arlene over you, he must be nuts. Look, I'll see you tomorrow, okay? Jason's picking me up in an hour and a half, and I've got to get my homework done first."

"Yeah, okay." She watched her friend hurry down the road before she crossed the main street to her own house. At school, she felt so humiliated she couldn't even look at Ronnie. Obviously he didn't want to date her. Otherwise he would've jumped at the chance, just like everyone else.

This was probably just something a popular person had to learn to live with, she figured. But it gnawed at her and in the days that followed she discovered that she wasn't as thrilled with the idea of being popular as she was before. She compared it to one of those "the-grass-is-always-greener-on-the-other-side-of-the-fence" type of things, where you dream of something for so long that the real thing can never compare with the picture you have formed in your mind.

Being popular meant to Frannie being somebody else three-quarters of the time. Being excited about an all-night football discussion when she was really bored stiff. Spending the evening at a Science Fair when she would have preferred to be watching a good movie. Or going to a party where she didn't know a single person except her date and trying to make interesting conversation.

Maybe she was being immature by thinking it should be any easier than it was. But at the same time, Frannie asked herself, why should I have to play a role? If I'm really compatible with somebody, somewhere, shouldn't conversation come naturally, without force?

"Here, use this stuff. It works pretty good." Ronnie Schell set a can of mechanic's hand cleaner in front of Frannie. She was having trouble getting the oil paint off her fingers. When she turned to face him, her eyes shone. "Oh, thanks a lot," she breathed, relieved and ecstatic that he had spoken to her.

"Mechanics use it to scrub the grease off their hands," he explained, smoothing the creamy gunk into his own palms. "Have you seen that new exhibit down at the city museum?"

"No, I haven't. But I'd like to. I hear the paintings are spectacular." Frannie's smile was quick and easy, not the pasted-on variety she'd been wearing at parties lately. Ronnie smiled back.

"Hey, Frannie." Adam Stone wedged himself between Frannie and the sink, where the gray bubbles from her hands oozed down the side of the porcelain.

"What?" She was of half a mind to flick bubbles at him, except he probably would have thought she was flirting with him, when she definitely wasn't. With all her heart, she wished he would go away!

Leaning so close Frannie could feel his breath

against her cheek, Adam said, "Let's go out this weekend, Frannie. I know you couldn't have a date yet."

Ronnie abruptly moved away from the sink. Her eyes met his for an instant, then he politely averted his gaze to concentrate on cleaning his brushes. She knew he could still hear the conversation, though.

"I—I don't think so," she stammered, her thoughts spinning insanely.

"Oh, come on babe," Adam persisted. "You know I'm obsessed with you."

"Stop joking around," was her terse, unsatisfactory reply. How she wished she could somehow explain this to Ronnie!

"You're such a tease, Frannie." Adam grinned at her, then swaggered off, his confidence unmarred.

Frannie's face was on fire. She hadn't handled that very well at all. Despairingly, she just knew Ronnie would never speak to her again after this. How she hated Adam Stone right now!

After school, Frannie declined a ride home with her friends to go to the school library instead. She needed some time to think, to be alone.

On the nonfiction bookcase there was a sculpture of a unicorn. Upon closer inspection, Frannie discovered it was made by Ronnie. Feeling proud for him, she traced a finger along the simple, uncluttered lines of the unicorn's body. How sensitive Ronnie was, and how admirable that quality is in a boy, Frannie thought. Nothing at all like Adam Stone, whom Frannie now knew to be downright pushy and obnoxious, not to mention conceited and arrogant.

Even the unicorn's eyes were beautifully formed, downcast lids with upswept lashes that conveyed an expression of "yes, I know I am beautifully made, but there are other things more so than I." Or maybe that was what Frannie thought Ronnie would say about his work. He never boasted about it, even though his talent was unique. Without a shadow of a doubt, she knew that on a date, Ronnie wouldn't monopolize a conversation with his amazing art feats and how wonderful Mr. Carniglia thought he was, although even if he did, Frannie would love to hear it. He would give her equal time, and would be interested in what she had to say, too.

But, oh, listen to me! she thought, and nearly laughed out loud. Dreaming again. Sure, Ronnie would listen to her—if he wanted to date her. Which he didn't.

With a weary sigh, Frannie patted the sculpture "goodbye" and strolled along the aisle until she located a book she wanted. After she had checked it out, she walked down the empty, echoing hallway of the main building, just savoring the quiet. She stopped to examine a couple of posters Ronnie had done for the upcoming Book Fair. There was one of a mouse rolled onto his back reading an oversized edition of Webster's Dictionary, and another of an old-time *Saturday Evening Post* magazine cover. Both were clever and showed a vibrant use of color and action. She'd love to talk to him about them someday.

Someday. The word had a heavy, leaden feel to it as Frannie rolled it around on her tongue. It was a word that wasn't really going anywhere. Her locker door slammed with a loud, metallic clank. Now that Adam had so rudely stepped between Ronnie and herself, she knew all her hopes and dreams of having Ronnie were completely dashed.

Chapter Seventeen

Gary drove with one hand on the steering wheel and the other holding Frannie's as he guided the car along the quiet, dark roads to her house. "Can you go out tomorrow night, Frannie?" he asked softly.

Frannie didn't answer right away. They had just been to a movie that Gary was crazy about. Frannie wasn't as thrilled, although she didn't say so. But perhaps that was because her mind kept meandering onto another subject all evening long— namely, Ronnie.

"I know you're probably busy," Gary went on. "Dudley's had your weekends pretty well sewn up, and you're not allowed out on weeknights..."

"I am going out with Cal tomorrow night, Gary. I'm sorry." She smiled at him in the darkness. If you were Ronnie, she thought, I'd cancel the date in a minute!

"That's okay. I think it's great you're dating other people. I mean, most girls want to get serious right away on the first date, and it's really a drag. They scare me off. It's more fun to go out with different people, don't you think? I don't like limiting myself." He swung the car into the driveway and leaned over for a goodnight kiss.

As his lips brushed hers, Frannie pictured

Ronnie's solemn face and imagined his kiss instead. How wrong Gary was about her! If only he knew how much she wanted a steady boyfriend. She was getting tired of these different dates with popular guys whom she was always trying to impress and who were always trying to impress her.

Gary walked her to her door, his arm around her shoulders. Frannie wished he was Ronnie—she wanted Ronnie's arms around her, Ronnie stroking her hair. "How about next Saturday night?" Gary whispered.

"Okay," answered Frannie, even though she was thinking how unfair it was of both of them to expect something else from each other.

"Dear Diary: Gary thinks I don't want a steady boyfriend and that I won't get serious like other girls he knows. Is that maybe what other boys think of me, too? Freddie does, but I figured that was because he liked me a little more than the others do.

"What I am and what they think of me are two different things. Wouldn't Gary drop me really fast if he knew how I really felt? Page would never ask me out again if he knew I'm not as interested in football as I've pretended to be, and the same probably goes for Cal.

"Saturday. Dear Diary: Today Cal and I went target shooting. I thought we were just going to shoot 'targets,' but it turned out that Cal wanted to shoot little birds. I was so upset, and I was afraid he would be upset with me if I didn't try just once, so I did. But I pointed the rifle just to

the side of the bird so I wouldn't hit it, and all the others flew away. Cal said I was a lousy shot, but I didn't care. All I cared about were those poor defenseless little birds. Why would a huge football player want to pick on such little creatures?

"I still feel just terrible. Cal and I were supposed to go out tonight with Charlene and Jason, but I called him and said I couldn't go. I just might stop going out with him altogether—even though he is the most popular guy in school. But can I afford to give up being popular?"

Frannie surveyed her calendar. The Plan had most certainly worked—the boys were now in a crazy competition for her time. Charlene had been so insistent that she accept as many dates as she could, especially with Cal. But now that she'd earned the popularity she so desperately wanted, couldn't she afford to be a little choosy?

What bothered her greatly was the kind of popularity she had earned. In most boys' eyes, she was just a nice, pretty girl who was fun to take out when you didn't have or want a serious girlfriend. But that wasn't at all what she wanted. If Gary and Fred saw her that way, there was a strong chance that Ronnie did, too.

"I hear you don't feel so good." After phoning Cal, Frannie wasn't too surprised to see Charlene, dressed in a striped red jumper and silky yellow blouse, ready to go out for the evening. "I thought I'd stop and see how you are, since you got sick so suddenly."

Frannie winced at the accusation in her tone.

"I told Cal when we were out before that I didn't feel good. Killing those birds really did make me sick."

"Big deal. All the guys do that."

Frannie studied her face, expecting to see Charlene's expression twisted into one of incredible cruelty, but instead she just smiled.

"Cal told Jason you didn't hit one anyway."

Frannie stared at her lap. "I shot away from the bird. I couldn't bear to kill it."

"It's just sport," said Charlene. "So what? Now come on and get dressed and go out with us."

"No, I'm not going, Charlene. In fact, I don't think I'm going out with Cal anymore. Anyone who shoots birds is not my kind of guy."

"You're crazy! He's nuts about you!" Charlene dropped onto the bed, wiping a fall of curls from her eyes.

"I want a real boyfriend, like you and Val and Patti have," she went on. "None of the boys I've dated are right for me. I always feel like I'm putting on an act for them. I'm not myself."

"I know Cal wants to go steady with you," Charlene urged.

"Didn't you hear me? I don't want Cal." Frannie took a deep breath. "Now that I'm popular, can't I choose somebody I like?"

"Ronnie!" Charlene fairly spat the name. "What a choice. We pick you the cream of the crop and all you want is this chump Ronnie." She scraped a lock of hair into a barrette. "The guys you've been dating are good enough for me or Val or Patti. Why not you? What makes you so special?"

"I'm not special!" protested Frannie. "Don't you see? But I want to be special to someone."

Clearly exasperated, Charlene jumped up and smoothed the front of her jumper. "I've got to go. But I still don't get it, Frannie," she said as she left.

Chapter Eighteen

Frannie was sick of Adam's constant teasing, especially in front of Ronnie. She cancelled her date with Gary, as well as the one with Page for Friday night. Finally, she turned down Cal, the boy Charlene considered Frannie's "ticket to popularity."

It didn't take long for this news to spread. By Tuesday afternoon, Patti, Charlene and Valerie were holed up in Frannie's room for another conference.

"I don't understand you, Frannie. You've got Mr. Wonderful eating out of your hand. Why don't you want him?" Patti exclaimed. She took a chocolate chip cookie from a plate on Frannie's dresser.

"Charlene says you want someone special. Well, Cal's special," Val said.

"He's not my type, Val," Frannie tried to explain. "Maybe I'm searching for some dream relationship, but I know I'm not going to find it with him. He'd be more interested in me if I were a football."

"Half the girls in school would give anything for him to say 'hi' to them and you say you don't want him! Are you playing hard-to-get, Fran?" Val inquired earnestly.

"No."

"Why not one of the others, then?" Charlene suggested. "You've been turning guys down right and left, and I know it's not because you've got your weekend lined up already." She was staring at Frannie's calendar, where Friday, Saturday and Sunday remained blank.

"None of the boys I date are right for me," Frannie said. "I know that sounds picky, but—"

"It sure does sound picky," snapped Patti.

"So you're turning them all down because they're not Mr. Wonderful?" Charlene asked point-blank.

It sounded so awful put that way, but it was true. "They all like me for the wrong reasons, and let's face it, the only reason I'm going out with them is because they're cute and popular."

"What better reason is there?" Val giggled.

Charlene told the others about Ronnie. "Look," Frannie began in her own defense, "The same boys you like don't have to be the ones I go for, do they?"

"What's wrong with our boys?" Patti asked. "Aren't they good enough for you?"

"Frannie, after all the work we put into making you a success, are you going to throw it all away? All the hours we spent making you beautiful, planning strategies, teaching you how to dance —does none of that mean anything to you anymore?"

"It does! You know I'm grateful for what you guys did," Frannie protested.

"Why can't you just date these guys until this Ronnie asks you out?" Val suggested.

"Because it wouldn't change my reputation at

school, Val," she answered. She had a feeling that Ronnie would never ask her out if she was still dating a lot of people. Just the way he acted when Adam asked her out that time in class demonstrated to her that Ronnie reacted differently to situations. He never joked about the incident as most boys would—he simply never brought it up.

"It's not what I want, though," Frannie said for what seemed like the thousandth time.

Charlene squeezed her temples with her fingertips. "I can't believe I'm listening to this! Ms. La-de-da doesn't want dates . . . Well, maybe, just maybe, you don't want us for friends, either."

"Yeah," chorused Patti.

"It sure sounds that way," agreed Val.

"No!" cried Frannie, but it was too late. The three girls marched out of the Bronson household, in spite of Frannie's protests.

After they left, Frannie sank into a depression. She put on a record to try to dispel the feeling, but it wouldn't leave. Instead, it tugged at her like an anchor, and she wished she'd never become popular at all. At least, when she was shy, she knew who she was.

Now she wasn't quite sure who—or what—she had become.

Of one thing she was sure: she wanted a different kind of popularity now. After all, she reminded herself, Ronnie took Arlene to Marilyn's party, and Arlene wasn't popular, so popularity must not be as important to Ronnie as it was to some boys. Frannie didn't want to be like Arlene exactly. She wanted to be herself and someone Ronnie would like—whoever that may be.

"Frannie, you're not going out tonight?" Mrs. Bronson's eyebrows rose in twin archs of concern.

"No, I don't have a date," explained Frannie. By most people's standards, the weekend might've been boring, but Frannie was glad for the opportunity to catch up on some old projects and to daydream.

Her mother settled on the couch beside her, and Frannie braced herself for one of their "heart-to-heart" talks. She pressed her sewing needle into a pin cushion and set aside her embroidery.

"Your friends haven't been by since Tuesday, and you haven't had a date all weekend," Mrs. Bronson remarked. "I was wondering if there was anything wrong."

"Nothing's wrong, Mom. I decided not to date as much, that's all. My friends are upset about it."

Her mother took her hand and rubbed it between her own. "How do *you* feel about it?"

"I liked dating a lot at first, but now I'm not excited about any of the boys I've been seeing. My friends don't understand that," Frannie told her guardedly. Even though they were pretty close, there was only so much she felt comfortable telling her mother. "I wish they wouldn't be mad at me, but there's nothing I can do." She explained a little about the boys she'd been dating. "I want to find somebody who's got something in common with me."

Her mother smiled. "Well, I hope the new somebody meets all your expectations," she said. Frannie got the distinct impression that her understanding ran deeper than her words.

"Mom, when I was dating a lot, you worried about me. Now that I'm not dating, you're still worrying about me. Don't you ever stop?"

"No. I'll always be concerned about your happiness," she said before disappearing into the kitchen.

With the phone silent and her parents gone for the day, Frannie spent that Sunday browsing through her diary and doing homework. In the past week, her entries had thinned out considerably.

"Monday. *Dear Diary: I stood next to Ronnie during clean-up. He said hello but I know he would say that to anyone who stood next to him. Adam put his arm around me in class, and I wish he would just leave me alone, which I've told him to do.*

"Wednesday. *Dear Diary: Today I saw Ronnie talking to Arlene at lunch. I'd have given anything to stand in her shoes. I sure would like to know what their relationship is.*

"Thursday. *Dear Diary: I wish the girls would speak to me, but they won't have anything to do with me. Cal phoned just to talk.*

"Friday. *Dear Diary: Ronnie was putting up posters for the Christmas Ball. They're more modern than the Halloween ones. I told him how much I liked them, but he just said thank you. I wonder if he thinks about me at all. Probably not."*

During the next weeks, Frannie's social life declined even further. At school, the talk was focused on the Christmas Ball and other pre-holiday events, and although Frannie was less forgettable than she had been prior to dating, she was no longer in the limelight. No one scrambled to sit by her in the auditorium during assemblies. She received few invitations out, and fewer phone calls than ever.

One afternoon after school she helped Fred move a whale vertebrae from his backyard into his station wagon. Afterwards, they drove to the school, where it would be displayed in the biology room. "I'm glad to see you're not so busy," Fred told her while they lifted the huge bleached bone out of the station wagon's bed.

"It shows?" Frannie was pleased Fred had noticed her change. She was careful, however, not to give Fred the slightest encouragement. He would get serious if only she gave the word.

The highlight of every day for Frannie was art, when she saw Ronnie. They rarely spoke, but when they did, it was always about something they were studying in class—color, shape, perspective. No amount of analyzing could dredge up the slightest hint of romance in their words, to Frannie's dismay. The one good thing to come out of it was that she found herself working harder at her art projects in the hopes of impressing him.

As the Christmas ball drew nearer, "Who're you

going with?" became the most frequently asked question. To which Frannie answered more than once, "No one."

Patti wagged her head in disgust at the news. "Still haven't nabbed your Prince Charming, huh? Why don't you give it up?"

Frannie blushed. She tried to smile, but it emerged as more of a grimace. "Have a good time, Patti," she said, yearning for a kind word from her one-time friend.

"Oh, you know I will." Patti launched into a detailed description of her dress, a slim-fitting crimson satin gown with crème lace lining the neck and sleeves. Frannie guessed Patti was tempting her to wish she were going, too—which it did.

But more than that, Frannie wished she could have a good, long conversation with her friends, a "conference" like they always used to have.

All too soon Patti announced, "Gotta go. Seeya around."

That was the kind of thing you said to someone you weren't very friendly with, Frannie considered, while desolation filled her heart. She watched Patti skitter down the hall into Scott's waiting arms. Students walking by edged out of their way, laughing.

At least if I can't have a boyfriend, thought Frannie, I should be able to have my friends. But it seemed as if her own decision had swept Patti, Charlene and Val's friendship up and almost out of Frannie's reach.

Chapter Nineteen

It seemed like a century since Frannie had gone to a movie all by herself.

"Be right out front waiting for me," her father reminded her before driving off.

"I will," she assured him and waved.

Her parents' suggestion to take in a movie had been a good one. Frannie couldn't bear the thought of sitting at home tonight, the night of the Christmas Ball. She knew herself well enough to know that it was better for her to be immersed in an exciting movie than to dwell on what was going on at the dance. Whatever happened, she was bound to find out about it at school Monday, anyway.

The line outside was half its usual size, probably because most of the high school students were at the dance. Frannie chose a seat in the middle, not wanting to be near the kissing couples who always took the seats in the far back.

Fortunately, the first half of the double feature, a spy movie, was as exciting as the ads promised, and Frannie found herself happily absorbed in the tightly woven story. At intermission, she joined the line at the concession booth with a smile of satisfaction on her face.

"Enjoy the movie?"

Startled, Frannie turned around to see who had spoken. The press of the crowd made it difficult to move. "Ronnie . . . hi." The smile broadened as she struggled to remember what he'd just asked her. "The movie was great, wasn't it?"

He grinned and swept a long-fingered hand through his dark hair. "Yeah. It's one I've been looking forward to for a long time. Movies take forever to get to this town."

Frannie nodded, her heart throbbing so fiercely she feared it might burst out of her chest. She inched closer to the booth, with Ronnie directly behind her.

"Who're you with?" Ronnie inquired. His eyes were a smoke-gray, thickly framed by dark lashes.

Frannie found it difficult to keep from staring at him. "I—I'm by myself. How about you?" His question seemed natural, hers seemed nosy, she felt.

"I'm with my brother, Paul. I told him to sit tight until I got back with the snacks."

"How old is he?" Frannie asked, secretly relieved he wasn't with a girl.

"Ten—a little stinker, too. My folks wanted him out of their hair tonight, and I wanted to get out, so I volunteered." He shrugged and shoved his hands in his jacket pockets.

"You must be a nice guy," Frannie giggled. "I don't have any brothers or sisters, but I hear enough complaints from my friends."

"You're lucky."

Mechanically, Frannie ordered popcorn and a Coke. Ronnie was so close, his ski jacket made a swishing sound against her velour sweater, and as he reached in front of her to grab a fistful of napkins, his hand accidentally brushed against hers.

"Excuse me," he apologized. "The kid's a real mess. I've got to have an arsenal of napkins."

Like an electric shock, Ronnie's warmth passed from the point of contact up Frannie's arms, making her tingle all over. Her hand trembled slightly when she reached for her Coke. If only he realized what an effect he had on her! "Oh, that's okay," she replied quickly.

Remember, she warned herself, he turned you down and took Arlene to Marilyn's party. She checked her feelings, hoping that her face didn't betray her happiness at meeting Ronnie so unexpectedly.

"Hey, you think we can sit together?" he asked.

Frannie's excitement perked. "Sure." I'll wait until you get your order."

Balancing drinks and popcorn, they shuffled back through the crowd to their seats. "You get my bonbons, Ronnie?" a child's voice piped.

Frannie looked down to the small, indignant-looking replica of Ronnie—the same gray eyes, the dark brown hair, the narrow, solemn face. "Hi, Paul," she greeted him.

Paul's gaze shifted from Frannie to his brother. "Who's this? How does she know my name? Where'd you find her?" He made a grotesque face and said, "Hi."

Ronnie turned to Frannie. "See, I told you he was a stinker."

Frannie had often longed for a younger brother or sister, even though her friends assured her they were more trouble than they were worth. But they never understood how lonely it was sometimes for an only child. To her, Paul didn't seem so bad.

"Is she going to sit with us?" Paul asked of Ronnie.

"Yes, now cool it, will you? Don't be impolite," ordered Ronnie, as Paul spilled buttery popcorn into his lap.

Frannie suppressed a laugh. She guessed that Paul was showing off on her behalf, and to embarrass his big brother, which he was doing very nicely as she could see by the color on Ronnie's ears. It was comforting to find that he blushed as easily as she did.

"Did you come to the movie all by yourself?" Paul inquired.

"Yes. I wanted to see this movie a lot, and I didn't have anyone to go with," explained Frannie.

"A pretty girl like you?"

Now it was Frannie's turn to blush, but she countered it with laughter. "Yes, a pretty girl like me."

Ronnie let out a sigh of relief when the second feature started. "Let's hope the movie holds his interest, because then it'll hold his tongue, too."

The second feature was another spy film, but not quite as engrossing as the first one. Ronnie and Frannie sat side by side, with Paul sitting next to his brother. Frannie didn't realize how much little kids squirm when they're supposed to sit in one place for a long time. Ronnie kept putting Paul in his place, in typically brotherly fashion.

Frannie sneaked a glance sideways at Ronnie's strong profile, lined by the smoky light filtered from the projector. Their shoulders touched ever so slightly, yet Frannie felt connected to Ronnie in an unexplainable, but wonderful way. Still, she cautioned herself not to get her hopes up. Just because they were sitting together at a movie didn't mean she and Ronnie were "together" in the dating sense.

Toward the middle of the film, Ronnie leaned close to her. "How are you getting home?" he whispered.

His breath against her ear gave her a pleasant shiver. "My father is picking me up," she replied softly, suddenly wishing he wasn't. On the screen, a couple was locked in a passionate embrace.

"Yuck—kissing!" exclaimed Paul, loud enough for a few people nearby to hear. Naturally, a few chuckles erupted around them.

"I'm glad no one can see who we are," Ronnie whispered, clearly embarrassed.

Frannie wondered if the theater had anything to do with the ease with which Ronnie talked to her. Clothed in the volume of the movie and separated from other people by the darkness, they enjoyed a privacy not found in the art room.

"Hey, I was surprised to find you by yourself tonight," Ronnie said.

"Why?"

"Why? Because you're always surrounded by guys, that's why. I thought you'd be at the Ball." He chuckled. "You're one of those popular girls who's generally unapproachable."

Frannie studied his shadowed face with surprise. "Gee thanks!" she responded, unsure whether to be hurt or to laugh.

"No, really. No offense, though," he added quickly. "I think it's a hangup of mine." Ronnie's sheepish smile told Frannie that everything was okay, and her excitement strained against the caution she'd imposed on herself.

The movie ended, and reluctantly, Frannie and Ronnie rose to leave. Paul pushed ahead of them. "Last one out's a rotten egg!" he chanted, weaving his wiry little body through the crowd.

Ronnie's hand stole over Frannie's. "Thank God for small favors," he said, winking at her.

They lingered for a few moments in the lobby, talking easily about art and other school events. Frannie looked outside where the bright beam of headlights swept across the entrance. "I've got to go. My dad will be waiting for me," she said regretfully. The last thing she wanted to do was leave Ronnie now, when she had dreamed of this moment for so long!

"Look, Frannie, are you doing anything tomorrow? I know you're really busy, but..."

Their eyes locked for a minute, in which Frannie became entranced by black flecks studded throughout the gray of Ronnie's pupils, and the sharp, but pleasant contrast of his dark hair and light eyes. "Uh, no, I'm not busy tomorrow," she stammered, breaking the spell.

"Could we do something? Have a picnic, maybe?" Ronnie squeezed her fingers, and the current travelled up her arm. She imagined it in her bloodstream, warming her from her toes to the tip of her nose.

"Sure, I'd like that." She smiled shyly. It was a little cool outdoors for a picnic, she thought, but leave it to Ronnie to come up with something unusual and different.

"I'll call you in the morning, okay?"

"Okay." Their fingers parted, and Frannie was aware of a cold draft between them, rushing through where the warmth had just been.

"Ronnie, you're a stinking rotten egg by now!" hollered Paul, thoroughly pleased with the embarrassment he caused his brother, as he scurried toward Ronnie.

"Cool it, Paul," grumbled Ronnie, his face noticeably flushed as he looked past his little brother to Frannie. "See if I ever take you anywhere again."

"Bye, Paul," called Frannie. "See you again."

"Bye!" Paul waved. Immediately he turned back to Ronnie and asked in a loud voice, "Will we see her again, Ronnie, huh?"

Right then, Frannie spotted her father waiting impatiently out in front, so she couldn't wait to hear Ronnie's answer.

"So how was the movie, Fran?" her dad wanted to know as soon as Frannie had settled herself in the front seat.

"Oh, great, Dad."

Frannie smiled a secret smile. If anyone asked her, she could describe the first movie in great detail, but all she could remember about the second movie was Ronnie sitting beside her.

Chapter Twenty

Was it all a dream? Frannie asked herself when she awoke Sunday morning. Her room was the same. Sunlight slanted through her bay window and picked out the dust particles floating in the air. Her clothes lay in an untidy pile on the carpet, and the quilt had slid off the bed during the night. But somehow, everything looked brand, spanking new, like the way the world looked after a long rain.

Thinking about last night (and she could think of nothing else), Frannie reached for her diary. But then she changed her mind. It was too early yet to record her feelings. They were so new, so fragile. She feared that writing about them might dispel the magic. And, too, what if Ronnie didn't call today, as promised? Then how would she feel?

So that she wouldn't be in the middle of something when and if he did call, Frannie dressed quickly, tiptoed into the kitchen, plugged in the coffee and waited near the phone, willing it to ring. She hoped he'd call early, before her parents got up, so they could have a private conversation.

It didn't work out that way, however. During her second cup of coffee the phone rang, and Frannie jerked and spilled the coffee down her front. Her mother was already up frying eggs and bacon, engaged in a discussion with her father about local politics.

Frannie breathed a sigh of relief when she heard Ronnie's voice. Thank God he wasn't just a dream! Even though it was quite brisk outdoors, they decided on a day at the beach. The excitement Frannie had reined in so tightly burst its bonds after she hung up the phone. "I'm going on a picnic today!" she sang.

Her parents acknowledged her with surprise. "With who?" they chorused.

"Ronnie Schell." The name rolled so easily off her tongue. Frannie yanked open the refrigerator to review the possibilities. "And now, I must make a picnic lunch, for two."

"Be sure to dress warm, now," her mother cautioned.

Clouds, like the tattered sails of ships, wafted across a cobalt-blue sky, and beneath it, a few figures scoured the beach in search of firewood.

Frannie and Ronnie spread a plaid wool blanket down near some high rocks, which would guarantee them a windbreak. Ronnie helped set everything up, and Frannie was glad that he didn't expect her to do all the preparation just because she was a girl.

"If we're both going to enjoy the day, we both have to pitch in," was how Ronnie had it figured.

Before lunch, they strolled along the beach together, talking.

"You know, I've been wondering why you didn't go to the Christmas Ball," Ronnie commented.

The wind blew his dark hair straight up and gave his cheeks a fresh ruddiness that Frannie had never seen on him. His eyes searched hers for an answer. "No one asked me," she replied honestly.

"I find that hard to believe. I mean, you're so popular, a guy would have to fight a crowd to date you." He grinned down at her.

"Correction, I used to be popular." She held up her index finger, but quickly stuffed it back in her warm pocket. "I sort of . . . gave it up."

Ronnie stopped and kicked at a mound of tangled seaweed. "Gave it up? How do you do that?"

It seemed unreal to relate to Ronnie what had for so long been thoughts she had confided only to her diary. But today, enclosed in their own little world within the vast expanses of sea and sand, the time was right to reveal a little something about herself.

"I felt like I was a phony, somebody other than myself. The boys I dated liked me for being that other person, and that just didn't feel right. Know what I mean?"

Ronnie nodded and urged her to go on. "I also saw that I was going out with them just because they were popular, and not because I liked them all that much."

"Boy, am I relieved to know that. Those big jocks are pretty stiff competition for a little guy like me."

Frannie laughed. "Not really," she assured him. "They're not my type at all."

"Tell me. What is your type?"

She guessed by the playful glint in his eye that

he was teasing her, but still, she suddenly became shy. "I'm trying to find that out," she replied softly. He laughed.

"When I saw you at Marilyn's party, I wished I could've accepted your invitation. I wished I was with you," he confided. "You looked really great—still do, of course." The color in his cheeks deepened.

Her hair blew across her face and with two fingers, Ronnie gently lifted it out of the way. "I like whatever it is you've done to change yourself, Frannie. I don't think you're phony at all."

She giggled, knowing that if she'd never learned to talk to boys, she wouldn't be standing here talking to Ronnie. "Speaking of Marilyn's party, I was pretty surprised to see you there with Arlene Paine," Frannie stated, holding her breath in anticipation of what he would say next.

"I live next door to Marilyn and she invited me, so I asked Arlene," he explained. "She and I have been friends since grade school, so it seemed like a safe date. I'm not real experienced at dating, you know. Nobody seemed just right to me. Until you, that is . . ."

The wind dried Frannie's smile to her teeth and whipped her hair into tangles, but she couldn't care less. What showed on the outside could not compare with the exultation she experienced within. Hand in hand, they trudged up the beach to eat their lunch, which Frannie noted, did not have much taste when you were falling in love.

"Try my potato salad," Ronnie offered. "I make fabulous potato salad."

Frannie took a dainty bite of the salad. It was

good. She decided not to tell Ronnie she didn't know how to make potato salad at all. Her expertise in the kitchen was limited to sandwiches and frying eggs. "Try my ham and cheese sandwiches," she suggested. "I make great ham and cheese sandwiches."

Ronnie agreed that she did. He ate so voraciously, Frannie doubted that he felt the same about her as she did about him. Her stomach was doing delicate, butterfly acrobatics.

"Aren't you hungry?" he asked, shoving the last of a brownie in his mouth.

"Not very." She picked up the litter of plastic containers and sandwich wrappers and put them in the picnic basket.

"What you need is a good run down the beach." Ronnie reached for her hand, and before she could resist, he had her on her feet, racing along the damp sand behind him.

That enigmatic boldness that Frannie had glimpsed only in Ronnie's vibrant painting was now very evident in his personality. What she had thought was contradictory and puzzling was simply another dimension of the same, fascinating Ronnie.

On one side, the sea pounded in rhythm to their footsteps. A stiff breeze nudged the two from behind, kicking up tiny whirlpools of sand. They ran until their sides ached and they couldn't catch their breath, even to laugh at themselves.

"Enough!" cried Frannie, doubling over onto the sand.

Ronnie collapsed beside her. "Don't you want to run back the way we came?" he asked, grinning. His hair flopped untidily over his eyes, but he looked good that way to Frannie.

"No, thanks. Why don't we take a taxi?"

They laughed. Ronnie leaned over and looked intently into her face. His gray eyes had often seemed cold and distant, but now they generated instant warmth when they met Frannie's.

Arms entwined, they slogged slowly back along the sand, stopping occasionally to point something out to each other. Frannie thought how like a scene from one of her father's commercials this day was. Yet it was real-life—something you'd paste in a scrapbook, if only you could capture it.

"I'd like to bring an easel down here and paint," Ronnie said.

"I was just thinking about capturing this scene." Frannie gazed out to sea, noting the bluish-green opaqueness of the waves as they crested, just before they plunged into a foamy spray. Etched on the horizon were a couple of fishing trawlers and several sailboats taking advantage of the wind.

Suddenly, Ronnie's arms stole about her waist. He drew her to him and kissed her, tentatively at first, then long and passionately. Frannie closed her eyes and concentrated on his tender, caressing touch, satisfied that at last, this was Ronnie, and no one else.

Her body pressed close to his, she thought, finally, all those impossible-sounding dreams are blossoming into reality.

Chapter Twenty-one

Frannie dropped her books on the lunchroom table and climbed into the seat next to Charlene. "You're going to listen to me, or else." She held up a small, but firm fist.

Charlene, Patti and Val stared at Frannie in mute disbelief. Val even set down her chopped olive sandwich to listen.

"I want you all to know how much I value our friendship. I still do, you know, even though I don't know if you still want me for a friend." Frannie averted her gaze from theirs, took a deep, quavering breath, then continued. "I'll never forget what you did for me to get me to date and overcome my shyness. I know I was really impossible."

"You've got that right," Charlene added sarcastically.

"No, let me talk. I needed all that crazy practice dating and dancing, and I'd still be a real mouse if it weren't for you, so I guess I owe you my life, in a sense." Frannie paused, partly for emphasis, and partly because she feared she might be getting too dramatic. Charlene rolled her eyes as though she were already exasperated with Frannie's speech, but Frannie couldn't worry about that now. She had to say what she came to tell them.

"But I don't need to be the most popular girl in school to be happy. I was what you'd call too popular for my own good. The plan worked so well that I had a reputation for not wanting to be tied down, and I don't think any of you would like a reputation like that. You all have steady boyfriends, you know.

"Ronnie and I are dating now." She couldn't say Ronnie's name without smiling. "And if it wasn't for you, we might never have gotten together at all, because by ourselves, both of us are so shy we could never start a conversation!"

Val giggled.

"So." Frannie cleared her throat. "I just wanted to stop by and say thank you. I really appreciate what you did for me." During the hush that followed, she lifted one leg, then the other, over the bench of the table and stood up to leave.

"Fran." Charlene's tear-filled eyes met hers. "Sit down."

"Yeah, sit down, Frannie," Val said softly, motioning toward the bench.

"Look, we didn't understand you, okay?" Patti offered a weak smile. "You acted so crazy, but I guess that's because you're in love."

"Do you still want to be friends?" Charlene asked. She dabbed her eyes with a tissue.

Frannie giggled. "Sure I do. I miss you guys."

"We've missed you, too. Even if you are crazy," Val laughed.

Ronnie waved to Frannie from across the cafeteria. "Hey, I'll see you later. I've got to go," she told her newly reinstated friends.

Charlene caught sight of Ronnie then. He was

leaning some posters up against the table edge. "He must really be something, Fran," she said, surveying him with new interest.

Frannie turned and winked coyly at her friend. "He is." Then she skipped across the cafeteria to meet him.

Nothing makes a summer special like falling in love ...

P.S. I LOVE YOU

Barbara Conklin

When her father left after the divorce, Mariah lost her sense of family. Now she's lost her special summer, too. Instead of fulfilling her dream to become a writer, Mariah has to help her mother with a house-sitting job in very rich, very snobby Palm Springs. People with a lot of money make Mariah uncomfortable.

Until she meets Paul Strobe, the rich boy next door. Paul's not a snob and doesn't act superior. In fact, his sandy hair and piercing blue eyes break down all Mariah's defenses. With Paul, Palm Springs becomes the most romantic place on Earth.

But Paul has to go into the hospital for some tests and then an operation. He's seriously ill and all his family's money can't help him.

Will Mariah lose Paul, too, just when she's found her first love?

0 553 20323 1   65p

A SELECTED LIST OF
BOOKS PUBLISHED BY CORGI

CHOOSE YOUR OWN ADVENTURE

☐	20892 6	1: The Cave of Time	*Edward Packard*	75p
☐	14003 5	2: Journey Under the Sea	*R. A. Montgomery*	75p
☐	14005 1	3: By Balloon to the Sahara	*D. Terman*	75p
☐	14000 0	4: Space and Beyond	*R. A. Montgomery*	75p
☐	20961 2	5: The Mystery of Chimney Rock	*Edward Packard*	75p
☐	14002 7	6: Your Code Name is Jonah	*Edward Packard*	75p

SWEET DREAMS

☐	20323 1	P.S. I Love You (72)	*Barbara Conklin*	65p
☐	20325 8	Popularity Plan (72)	*Rosemary Vernon*	65p
☐	20327 4	Laurie's Song (72)	*Suzanne Rand*	65p
☐	20328 2	Princess Amy (72)	*Melinda Pollowitz*	65p
☐	20326 6	Little Sister (72)	*Yvonne Greene*	65p
☐	20324 X	California Girl (72)	*Jane Quin-Harkin*	65p

*All these books are available at your bookshop or newsagent, or can be ordered direct
from the publisher. Just tick the titles you want and fill in the form below.*